"Remember, we're pretending that this is a real date."

In reply, Robbie's heart began to pound as they neared her front porch. "Come on, Jason," she said nervously. "You really don't have to see me to the front door."

Jason stopped abruptly and drew her around to face him. "All right," he said, "let's drop the pretence, shall we? Let's be truthful and tell each other what we feel. Are you ready for that?"

He made her feel so strange. He was full of a tension she couldn't understand. She couldn't tell him what he was making her feel...the trembling he caused in her. "I don't know what you're talking about," she whispered.

He drew her nearer with a gentle, inexorable insistence. "That's one of the few times you've ever lied to me."

AMANDA CARPENTER, who wrote her first Harlequin romance when she was nineteen, was raised in South Bend, Indiana, but now lives in England. In her romance novels Amanda endeavours to enhance their quality with original story lines and an individual style. When she's not writing, she pursues her interests in art, music and fashion.

Books by Amanda Carpenter

These books may be available at your local bookseller.

Don't miss any of our special offers. Write to us at the following address for information on our newest releases.

Harlequin Reader Service
901 Fuhrmann Blvd., P.O. Box 1397, Buffalo, NY 14240
Canadian address: P.O. Box 603,
Fort Erie, Ont. L2A 9Z9

AMANDA CARPENTER

waking up

Harlequin Books

TORONTO • NEW YORK • LONDON
AMSTERDAM • PARIS • SYDNEY • HAMBURG
STOCKHOLM • ATHENS • TOKYO • MILAN

Harlequin Presents first edition October 1986
ISBN 0-373-10919-9

Original hardcover edition published in 1986
by Mills & Boon Limited

CHAPTER ONE

LAZY warmth, on a peaceful summer day. Lazy, sensuous warmth. With her eyes closed, Robbie could see a blurry red as the sun's hot, powerful rays pulsed down on her lithe, outstretched body. Clad in the briefest of swimsuits, she oozed sleek, shiny, slippery suntan oil, every browned muscle relaxed, full mouth slightly curved in unspoken satisfaction.

The air smelled like freshly cut grass, the fruit of her recent endeavour. It was a ritual for Robbie to cut the grass every Saturday during the summer, weather permitting. Her father worked quite hard, and she always felt that it was his due to have at least one day in which he could totally relax, with no obligations to meet. She raised slim arms over her head in a languid pose and sighed, turning her head to one side. Someone else in the comfortable neighbourhood was cutting grass; the sound of a mower purred and rattled, a continuous, faint undercurrent to the occasional passing car and the far-off shouts of children playing.

The sound of quiet footsteps came to her, along with the impression of something large approaching, and Robbie tensed very slightly. She waited, the serenity of her afternoon splintering. The footsteps stopped just beside her lounge chair, and after a moment's stillness, the person folded down into a sitting position.

She knew who it was and waited for him to speak first, for she was still too full of resentment to make the first overture. Jason said quietly, deep voice blending mellow and rich with the other summer sounds, 'I spoke out of turn, yesterday. I'm sorry.'

Robbie rolled on to her stomach, a quick, tense movement, and hid her face in her arms. After a moment, she spoke and the words throbbed with hurt. 'You felt what you said. You still do.'

A heavy sigh came from him. 'Not really. You were right. Nobody other than you can know what's best for you. I still don't like the thought of all your energy and talent going to waste in that waitressing job of yours, but then it isn't any of my business. If you're happy that's the most important thing.'

She raised her head, light brown hair blowing across her eyes and obscuring Jason's features. 'I have to take things at my own speed,' she said. 'I have to do what I want to do, not what you or someone else wants. You've done so well for yourself that you want everyone else to know the same kind of satisfaction and success, but it just doesn't work that way.'

Her brown eyes met his, which were a light, silvery grey, clouded now with a frown. 'I know,' he said gently, his gaze steady and apologetic. Jason was always very good about that. He apologised handsomely, with integrity. A slow smile spread across his lips creasing his lean face. 'You just be happy, Rob. That's all I ask.'

She relaxed and grinned back, laying her head down with a plop. 'I'd be happier if I had something cold to drink right now,' she said pathetically, and he snorted.

'Give her an inch, and she takes a continent. All right, I'll go and get you something. Is your back door open?'

'Yup,' she said to her forearm and listened as he stood and walked away. She called out, 'Help yourself to a beer, if you like.'

Robbie hated beer, and Jason well knew it. But her father liked the drink, so they usually kept a six-pack in the refrigerator during the summer.

There were a lot of little things like her dislike of beer that Jason knew about her, and her father. She had grown up with Jason and his family. He lived just next door to them, in a rather secluded cul-de-sac that held just three houses. In the third house lived an older, childless couple, so she and Jason had gravitated towards each other from the start. He was twenty-four, two years older than she, and already doing well for himself. He had earned his undergraduate degree in business administration, and he already made a substantial salary as a junior executive in a local branch of a nationwide public accounting firm. He had drive, but he'd always been that way, ever since she was ten and he was twelve.

And so now he was destined to go places, with enough ambition to make his career soar. He had all his future ahead of him, and she was as proud of him as if he'd been her own brother. Looking at his possibilities was extremely exciting, but Jason simply had to learn that he was no longer the leader, and that her life would branch in ways that his would never do, that she had to find her own ambitions and her own life's desire.

That was what they had argued about, last night. Since he had started college six years ago, the close, best-friend relationship that they had shared had cooled. She hadn't seen him for months at a time when he had gone away to attend university, and then she'd seen him very briefly. He was busy during the summers at the different jobs he'd acquired, while she was busy with her own life, dating, working at a twenty-four-hour family restaurant and later, after she'd become old enough to obtain a liquor licence, at a distinguished, elegant restaurant. Then Jason had graduated at the top of his class and instead of trying his luck in one of the larger cities, which had been what everyone had expected, he had chosen to come back to Cincinnati to live for the time being.

And he was back, however infrequently, in her life. He found a large, lovely apartment across town, close to his work, and she saw him about as much as she had when he was at college. That was, until last week. He had moved back home for the summer to keep an eye on the house while his parents, who had recently retired, took an extended vacation in Europe.

It had seemed like old times when he had wandered over, yesterday evening, as she sat with her father in the front garden and looked over the deserted side street, talking over their respective days. Jason had sprawled at his ease on the ground at their feet, and while her father was outside, their visit had been companionable. She had felt a real surge of pleasure at his presence along with that old, half-exasperated affection she'd always felt for him. It had been good old Robbie and Jason again.

But when her father had finally risen from his chair to go inside, the conversation between herself and Jason had gradually, subtly changed. She still couldn't pin-point where it had occurred. Soon it dawned on her that they were arguing, and not in the old foolish way of the past. (Did so. Did not. Did so.) It had been an argument of strange strength and incomprehensible motivations, until she had felt pressured into crying out, 'You are a fine one to talk of my lack of ambition! If you're so full of it, why did you come back here instead of moving to New York, or Los Angeles? You could have made it big, could still do it. Why are you here?'

She hadn't meant it as anything but a diversion from herself. At the very least, she'd simply wanted to point out that he wasn't in a position to be giving her unwanted advice. But he had reacted strangely in a strange argument, going quite quiet and still as he sat at her feet and ignored her father's now-empty lounge chair. His long, muscular legs were stretched out and one shoulder flexed as he leaned back on his hand. Something in Jason's grey eyes flickered as he looked at her and then away, as if to hide the expression in them. 'I . . . have family here,' he said softly. She couldn't think why he had hesitated over the words.

'Well, just don't tell me how to live my life,' she had said then, her face closed tight and full of resentment. 'It's not wanted or needed, d'you hear?'

It had been an odd, disturbing occurrence. They

had both reacted in ways that perhaps they shouldn't have. If she hadn't been so sensitive about the subject already, then maybe she wouldn't have been so defensive, for surely he had the best of motives in wanting to encourage her. Ah, well. It was best forgotten.

She heard the back door slam a second time and knew that Jason was returning. He walked over to her, and then she felt something extremely cold trickle wetly down her heated back. She reacted as if she'd been scalded, yelping and leaping straight up in the air, landing beside the lounge chair and rounding on him furiously.

He stood with one slim hip leaning against the chair, legs long and deeply tanned under brief, ragged cut-offs, chest bare and dark, teeth flashing white as he laughed openly at her. In one hand he held an open beer can, and in the other, a sweating glass of iced lemonade. After sputtering like a faulty motor for a few moments, she reached grumpily for her drink and subsided back into her chair, sending him one last, glowering look. It bounced off his thick hide.

He settled at her side, squinting up at the afternoon sun. He, too, had light brown hair, but his was several shades lighter than hers, with golden highlights brought out by the summer sun. He was a lean young man, standing just under six feet, with tight, compact muscles, thickened shoulders as he had reached maturity, and keen, steady grey eyes under sleek brows. She ran her eyes over him appreciatively. He would age well, with perhaps a deepening of lines at the corners of his eyes in twin spreading fans, and a sprinkle of white at his temples. He stretched, lithe as a cat, and threw her a lazy smile as he said casually, 'Lusting after my beautiful body?'

'Mmm,' she replied, disparagingly, and then laughed as he cocked a pained eyebrow at her response. She continued wickedly, 'Oh, yes, you are a cute young thing, ripe for some forty-year-old, man-hungry divorcée to snap up.' She reached over and held her half-empty glass over his flat, sleek stomach, dribbling cold liquid on him.

His reaction was much the same as hers had been, only surprisingly faster. He thrust her hand away with a grumbled curse. 'Now, stop that before I pour the rest of this beer in your hair. Forty-year-old divorcée, eh? Would she be rich?'

'Definitely.' Robbie sat her drink precariously in the grass and settled back, stretching her arms over her head and closing her eyes against the bright glare of the sun. She felt a tickling drop of sweat slither down her chest. 'She'd sweep you off your feet and demand that you leave your job. Then she'd keep you in her guest bungalow by the beach. You'd sneak up to the main house in the night and lie in the sun by day, drinking those fruity concoctions that hit you like an exploding bomb.'

'Ye Gods.' His reply was not particularly indicative of any worry. 'I'd have a paunch by the time I was thirty, be kicked out after she tired of me, and be unable to find a decent job because I'd lost touch with the market. No, thank you.' The last was with some degree of dryness.

Robbie raised her head slightly to look at him. She was hot, and as always when she grew so heated, she felt an overwhelming reluctance to move any part of her body. She shifted her legs, feeling them slip along the lounge cushion, and knew she'd have to hose down the chair to rinse off the suntan lotion. 'You don't like the older sophisticate? Well then, you'll probably find yourself some sweet young virgin, fresh out of high school, and spend the rest of your life having the little woman take care of you.'

He winced, exaggeratedly. 'I already have a doormat and I have no overriding desire to have someone running all day long to cater to my needs, for God's sake. Can't you imagine some other, less stifling future for me?'

She pondered that. 'You'll be a free, swinging bachelor, with bags under your eyes from years of late nights and affairs begun in singles bars,' she offered sleepily and laughed at his groan.

'Speaking of late nights,' said Jason then, as he sat and drank the rest of his beer, 'are you working tonight?'

Robbie smiled. 'Nope. I've got a date.'

'Oh, yes?' he said, and laughed. She frowned at him heavily. 'What's he like?'

This was a great deal like the way they had treated each other through high school. He had treated everyone that she dated with the same tolerant scorn that she had shown for his choices. He had also shown a remarkable patience whenever she found herself crying out her broken heart at the end of a particularly nasty break-up, and similarly, she had stifled her own impatience when he talked endlessly about the virtues of his current goddess.

But now she didn't feel like pouring out her youthful heart, and for a reason she couldn't begin to fathom, she shrugged his question aside carelessly. 'Oh, heck. When you've seen one, you've seen them all, know what I mean?'

That made him laugh out loud, and the sound of it rolled over the lawns. 'God! You are to the morale what the Japanese were to Pearl Harbor! When did you pick up that nasty trait?'

She flicked up a hand to tuck her shoulder-length hair out of her eyes. 'It comes with age, my dear,' she said, wearily. 'It comes with age.'

Jason got up on his knees and bent over her. She squinted up at him, ostensibly irritable, and found herself vaguely uncomfortable because she couldn't see his facial expression. All she could see, half-blinded, was the black outline of his head and strong, naked shoulders, and then she sat up and rubbed her eyes to dispel the illusion. He was still inspecting her closely, too closely. 'What are you doing?'

It was his turn to shrug. 'Just checking for the bags under your eyes,' he replied, sweetly.

He stayed for a few more minutes, though they didn't talk much. Then after a while, he rose, told her to behave herself, to which Robbie didn't deign to reply, and as he walked away, she turned her head to watch.

Jason broke into an easy, hip-swinging lope and then gathered his lean body and leaped over the thigh-high fence which separated the Morrows' yard from theirs. It was one fluid, athletic motion, and she briefly, dispassionately admired his animal grace. Then she grinned reminiscently. She could remember how proud she'd been of herself when she had finally screwed up enough courage to try to leap that fence. Jason had bet her a dollar that she couldn't, to which she had responded with gritty determination. Afterwards, when she'd cleared it by a good three inches, he had strutted around telling everyone, as pleased with her as if he'd done it himself.

The sun soon lost its attraction, for her eyes began to ache from the glare, and then started to throb, so she forsook the lounge chair to wander listlessly inside. There she poured herself another lemonade from a gallon pitcher and shook out a few aspirin which they kept in a cupboard. She downed them along with half the lemonade at one go. In the summer, she always drank lots of liquid and cut back on food, as she lost her appetite in humid heat.

The rest of the afternoon stretched ahead of her, with no energy or obligations to fill it. Her limbs felt heavy and slick with the oil, so she trod upstairs to shower with cool, refreshing water, which revived her somewhat. Then she made her way to her bedroom and sat in front of her large open window, brushing at her dripping hair.

Falling into a brood that afternoon seemed easy. Her lower lip thrust out slowly, and her sleek, well-defined brows drew together as her hand rose more and more slowly to run the brush through her thick, wet locks. Maybe Jason was right, and that was why he had upset her so much. Maybe she was unwilling to face her own future. She was already twenty-two years old. Jason had graduated the summer of his twenty-second year, with the security of knowing he already had a good job waiting for him. A lot of people with whom she had gone to high school were graduating from college and shooting off to find their dreams. And what was she doing with herself? Where was she heading?

Certainly, there was nothing wrong with waitressing. That simply wasn't the point. She liked it well enough, didn't dread going to work, and in four nights she could make well over three hundred dollars in tips. She didn't have to pay any rent as she still lived with her father, and though she helped with buying groceries, that expense was relatively minimal. All she did was go to work in the evenings, amuse herself during the day, date occasionally, and put her money in a bank account. Though she had a nice nest-egg built up, she had no goals, nothing to look forward to, not even an exotic holiday planned for herself.

Robbie sighed heavily and put her hair brush down on the window sill, hardly aware that she lined it up carefully with the sill's edge. This depression threatened to get serious. What she needed was something to spark her interest, something to liven up her life and put some zest back into her days. She needed something to make her feel feisty and mischievous, to bring back the Robbie she used to be.

The Robbie she used to be. That brought a wry, acknowledging twist to her lips. The tree-climbing, sarcastic, skinny little brat she used to be. She was still sarcastic. At least she wasn't quite as skinny any longer, having filled out slightly in places she thought she never would, though she was still quite slim. But somewhere the fire was gone, for there was nothing to get fired up about, these days.

She'd always been something of a crusader. When her father and she had first moved into the neighbourhood after her mother had died, she had gone around for months with a major chip on her shoulder. She had been angry with the world. She hated Ohio, and Cincinnati was putting insult to injury. She wanted to move back east, where all her friends were. The boy next door was a snotty-nosed kid who teased her at every opportunity and the school she had to go to was the absolute pits.

She was the new girl, the silent one, the girl who got teased, the outsider. Then one day at lunch-break, two girls and a boy had been giving her a hard time, with the hooting derision that only children could, while she tried desperately to ignore them and prevent herself breaking into tears. A sudden dusty whirlwind had descended on the four of them. It had been that insufferable brat, Jason, who chased the boy away and jeered at the two girls, saying such vile things that they ran off in embarrassment while Robbie had stood staring, speechless with admiration at his remarkably foul mouth. She could still remember how he had told her, very indifferently, that while he could and would tease her all he liked, nobody else would, and that was all there was to it.

They became a pair. When one thought up a scheme, the other always staunchly went along with it. Even when Jason left elementary school for Junior high, they got together in the afternoons. He taught her how to throw a deadly softball. One year they slipped outside late at night to get into mischief, and only got caught towards the end of summer. They made up secret codes and found extraordinary hiding places to put messages. They squabbled, made up with a studious disinterest, and fiercely stuck up for one another. They were best friends.

Femininity came late for Robbie. She was never Roberta, and most often just Rob. Without a mother's influence, her teens were rather painful and self-conscious, and she made a crusade out of ignoring boys and the girls who primped and preened for their attention. Jason was more important to her than she would have admitted to anyone. To Jason, she was just herself. He didn't give a hoot if she had dirt on her nose, scratches on her legs, or grass in her hair. Granted, he never commented on the rare occasions when she dressed up either, but that was what she had liked about him. He went away to school when she was sixteen, and only then did she begin to concentrate on learning how to look attractive to the opposite sex. Time trickled by.

That was the problem, she reflected broodingly. Time always seemed to be just slipping by, and she wasn't doing anything about it. She was just letting herself grow older.

She shook herself free of her introspection and checked her bedside alarm clock to find that she should have begun dressing some time ago. With a moan, she flew into action and scrabbled for her new light green summer dress, with the tailored waist and slim skirt. That, along with a severely cut white jacket in case the evening cooled later

on, and white, slim-heeled sandals was her outfit.
She let her straight brown hair swing free and
simple and emphasised the largeness of her dark
eyes with smoky shadow and mascara. That, along
with blusher on her cheekbones and lip colour on
her full lips, completed her toilet, and she hurried
downstairs as it was nearly six.

Her face being characterised by a pert nose and
strongly defined, sleek brows made her more
interesting and attractive rather than simply
beautiful, and she had tailored her wardrobe to
suit her lanky looks, going for sleek, streamlined
styles and severe cuts that emphasised her figure
best. As a result she was rather striking, and no
one was to know that she secretly deplored the fact
that she couldn't wear the froth and frills that
some women could.

Now that she was actually upon this evening,
having spent the afternoon in a somewhat glum
reminiscence, she was looking forward to her
date. She had to grimace briefly for she knew
that Jason wouldn't approve of the man she was
seeing, and that had been the reason why she
had been so reticent. Not that his opinion
mattered all that much to her. Oh no, it was just
that she knew Ian Walsh wasn't the kind of man
that Jason would have liked her to associate
with. Jason was simply going to have to realise
that she now made character judgments and life
decisions on her own.

She had teased Jason about being the free,
swinging bachelor type because she knew he didn't
like it. And, she had to admit, Ian probably fitted
that description as well as any man. But he was so

amusing, so interesting and lively and attentive, so damned good-looking that she couldn't resist going out with him. She liked him. He was dark, powerfully built, and in his early thirties, with a lovely, wicked smile that could charm honey away from killer bees. He also travelled a lot with his job, but he never failed to call her whenever he was in town, and she had been seeing him for a few months now. Her mood shifted even further, and she became quite cheerful. Tonight Ian was taking her out to eat, and as his taste was always impeccable, she knew that she could relax and look forward to the meal with enjoyment. Being a waitress herself, she appreciated being waited on. She had met Ian at work. He had dined at one of her tables one fine spring evening, and soon he seemed to be coming in every week. It was some time before the hostess told her that he had been requesting her station specifically. Close on the heels of that revelation, he had asked her out, and that was how she had started seeing him.

She went into the kitchen to see if her father had started any supper for himself and found spaghetti sauce bubbling away on the stove, so she stirred it. Then she hurried along the hall to the living room, hoping Ian hadn't arrived yet and was waiting for her.

Ian hadn't, but keeping her father company, while lounging comfortably on the sofa, was Jason, looking rather alien in clothes slightly more formal than the jeans and cut-offs in which she was used to seeing him. She stopped in surprise at seeing him and then advanced slowly into the room.

'What are you doing here?' she asked, not particularly worried about tact.

The twist of his well-cut lips showed that he was aware of it, but as he let his eyes travel in leisurely appreciation of her figure, he answered her in all seriousness. 'I'm keeping your father company for supper tonight.'

'Oh.' A moment while she digested this, shifting uneasily under his all too obvious stare, and then she looked to Herb Fisher, who was at his ease in his favourite armchair. 'Hi, Dad. How was the golf course?'

'Too damned crowded,' he grunted, and gave her a lopsided grin. 'But I was three under par, which made up for it.'

She gave a low whistle, while dropping her handbag to a nearby table. 'I'll say. Congratulations. I bet Jim Dennison was green with envy.'

Her father chuckled his satisfaction. 'He wasn't speaking much as we left the course, so I couldn't say.'

She laughed, and went over to the front window to check the driveway. As she let the curtain fall back into place, Jason said silkily, 'I can't wait to meet your date. He will come to the door, won't he?' His tone implied that he believed the worst.

She eyed him with disfavour. 'I was considering running out before he could,' she retorted, which made him grin, light grey eyes dancing merrily.

Their driveway was concrete all the way to the road, with no gravel to herald the arrival of a car. All she heard was a low purr just before the car's engine was turned off, and before she could stand to take her handbag and go out to meet Ian, he was getting out of the car and coming towards the house. Jason rose smoothly to his feet and beat her to the door, pure devilment sparkling in his eyes at her exasperation.

He opened the door and said cordially, 'Hello, won't you come in? You're Rob's date, I believe?'

Robbie stood back, smiling slightly as Ian looked at her from under his straight black brows and then back to Jason to smile coolly. 'Yes,' he agreed, his voice cultured and smoothly polite. 'I am.' He turned to Herb. 'Hello, Mr Fisher, how are you? You're looking good.'

'Thank you, sir,' said her father, lazily from his chair. 'I'm feeling good.'

Ian turned back to her and smiled, slow and sweet, into her eyes. She let her eyes twinkle back at him, while Jason stood back and observed them both dispassionately. 'Are you ready?' asked Ian, and she nodded, reaching for her bag.

'No need to leave, yet,' said Jason easily, and she could have turned around to kick him. Out of her sight, her father just settled back and looked on, as peaceful as a baby. 'Stay and have a drink.'

Ian let his eyebrows rise slightly as he looked to her for confirmation. She said firmly, 'I'm ready to go.'

'Then we'll be passing on that drink tonight,' said Ian to Jason, smiling wickedly. 'Good evening, gentlemen.'

As he held back to let her precede him, she couldn't resist throwing a glare at Jason for his behaviour, but she could have predicted the result. He raised his brows in bland, mocking reply behind Ian's left shoulder and let her glare bounce off him.

In the car, as Ian pulled out of the driveway, he said casually, 'By the way, who was that? Have I met him?'

She looked out of the passenger window so that he couldn't see her face. 'No,' she replied with a sigh. 'You haven't. He's our neighbour. I grew up with him.'

She could sense the appraising look he threw at her, along with the slightly amused smile that played on his refined lips. 'Odd fellow,' he said laconically.

'He's set himself up as my big brother for about ten years, now,' she told him, somewhat unfairly, and couldn't help but smile then. 'Please don't take offence.'

At that, he laughed. 'Oh, no. I would never do that. Your big brother, eh? How interesting.'

'What do you mean by that?'

'Nothing,' he said cheerfully. 'Absolutely nothing.' Then, with another of his lovely smiles, 'I hope you're hungry tonight. I find that I'm quite starved.'

She enjoyed the evening. Ian was his usual charming, attentive self. She laughed and said all the right things, and appreciated the good food and service. Maybe, she mused into her wine glass, maybe this was what was lacking in her life, an exciting, romantic man who stimulated her senses and pleasantly thrilled her with his attention.

The evening was balmy and clear, though windy enough for her to be thankful that she had thought to bring her white jacket. The stars were visible in abundance, and the trip back was made with low, soothing music played over Ian's excellent car-stereo. She allowed her head to loll back on the seat and her mind to roam dreamily. He pulled into her driveway, turned off the engine, and tilted his dark head towards her with a gentler version of that wicked smile. He reached out and took her hand, playing with her fingers. 'Thank you,' he said, and she looked startled, then laughed.

'Good heavens, Ian, that's supposed to be my line!'

'That may be, madam, but I enjoyed your company, so I thank you for it,' he retorted. She smiled back at him through the duskiness, feeling a bit uneasy for some odd reason. She waited patiently for the moment when she could draw her hand away without hurting his feelings or appearing rude. 'I want to see you next week,' Ian continued softly.

'That would be nice,' she replied as quietly. Why, for heaven's sake, was she feeling so self-conscious and uncomfortable? They had lingered like this many times before. She ran her gaze over the darkness of the house, knowing her father would have gone to bed long before.

'I'm going to be out of town for a while, but I'll give you a call when I get back, all right?'

'That sounds good,' she murmured, only half her attention on him.

Suddenly she knew why she felt uncomfortable. The lights in the front room at the Morrows' house were on, and apparently Jason was up late. She felt stupid at being bothered by that, but she was.

Ian drew near, bending his head slowly. He pressed his lips to hers gently, time and time again, tantalisingly brushing her mouth, one hand going to her long, slim neck to stroke lightly. She tried very hard to feel natural. Certainly she had responded normally, with pleasure, in the past. But her heart wasn't in it. It didn't feel right. She felt stilted and awkwardly shy.

Somehow she made it through decently enough and said her good nights. Soon she was locking the front door behind her and leaning against it with an explosive sigh. She felt like an idiot and fervently hoped that Ian couldn't tell that anything was wrong. She liked him too much and she wanted him to call back.

She thrust away from the front door and paced through the darkened first floor of her home restlessly, berating herself about how stupidly she had acted over a mere coincidence. As she passed through the kitchen, which faced the Morrows' house, she glanced out exasperatedly to the object of her frustration and stopped dead. She didn't know why it bothered her to find that the living-room light was off now and that the front of the house was quite dead. For a mere coincidence, it bothered her very much.

CHAPTER TWO

THE next morning, Robbie dragged herself out of bed reluctantly and dressed in ragged jean-shorts that had been washed so many times they were nearly white, along with a brief, light blue tank top that showed a great deal of her slim, dark brown arms and shoulders. Then she went downstairs to the kitchen. The house was already quite warm, hinting of the summer heat yet to come that day. She opted for a glass of orange juice and a glass of iced tea instead of her usual cup of coffee. She was a habitual late riser, since her job entailed late nights. It was sometimes as late as two o'clock before she went to bed, and so her days started at around nine or ten.

After sitting at the breakfast table and reading the Sunday paper, she rose to half-heartedly clean a few of the downstairs rooms, and then when she had appeased her conscience for the day, she found the paperback she was currently reading and went outdoors.

This time, instead of settling in the sun, she arranged the lounge chair under the shade of a mature maple tree and composed herself on it to enjoy a leisurely reading session.

Herb went to church every Sunday, and Robbie was hard put to decide whether the attraction was purely religious or if it had anything to do with the lovely widow who attended regularly and in whom her father had shown an increasing interest lately. She had fallen out of the habit of attending church when she had started her job; more often than not, she worked on Saturday evenings and found that after eight to ten hours of sheer, hard physical work, it was too hard to drag herself out of bed after only five or six hours' sleep.

Movement from the Morrows' lawn drew her gaze, and she looked over to see Jason clipping energetically at the long row of hedge that lined the house. He was dressed as he had been the afternoon before, in faded cut-offs which resembled hers and nothing else, his bare, broad shoulders flexing sinuously in rhythm as he worked the shears.

Though it was quite hot, he was relentless, and after a time she couldn't help but feel un-comfortable as she imagined the trickles of sweat that must be slipping down his torso, along with the ache in his upper arms. Perhaps he wouldn't feel it quite as much as she would, as he was obviously more powerful, but she put her book down anyway and ran lightly inside to pour him a glass of the iced tea she had made that morning. Then she strolled back outside and over to his lawn.

If he knew of her approach, he didn't show it, whistling soundlessly through his teeth as he worked. She watched him silently for a few moments, fascinated by the rippling display of sleek, well-honed muscle under the silken-smooth, dark skin. She couldn't believe how he had managed to become such a marvellously well-endowed male without her having realised it.

She almost put her hand out to stroke at the lovely, powerful back. Catching herself with an obvious start, she cleared her throat and said to him, 'Here, drink this before I have to watch you collapse with heat stroke.'

Jason spun around to face her, brows mildly raised. At the sight of the tall, frosted cold glass, his white teeth flashed quick and bright. 'Why thank you, sweetheart,' he said lightly, and took the glass from her to empty in one long, thirst-satiating drink. His head was tilted back, light brown hair tangled and falling from his strong forehead, long throat muscles working. Robbie's gaze slithered down his throat and then automatically went over the flat, broad expanse of his trim chest and waist. A very light sprinkling of silky hair salted that area, narrowing to a sleek arrow that plunged into his shorts, which were slung low on his slim hips.

Her glance skittered away, and she looked at his lean face and found him regarding her quizzically, questioningly, light eyes vivid. He cradled the glass in his long fingers and swished the ice cubes around. 'How was your evening last night?' he asked.

She shrugged and shifted her feet restlessly. 'It was fine,' she replied offhandedly. 'We ate out and had a leisurely drive back. It wasn't anything especially different, but it was quite nice.'

He nodded, and tilted his head sideways to squint up at the cloudless, brilliant sun-filled sky. With a great, heaving sigh, he raised one wrist to wipe his damp forehead and said, 'I must be out of my mind to be doing this now.' As she agreed

privately, he looked at her with a neat turn of his
head, and commented very casually, 'That Walsh
fellow is a bit older than you.'

Robbie had rather expected something like that
from him and she felt a flush of resentment rise to
her face, much to her annoyance. 'He's in his
thirties,' she said, the shortness of her tone a
warning.

Jason grunted and threw her a look from under
his level brows. Then he smiled unexpectedly. She
felt taken aback, as it was particularly sweet. 'He
seems like a nice man, Rob. Thanks for the tea.'

He handed her the glass with something of a
shove, as she murmured that he was welcome and
not to mention it, her fingers colliding with his
longer, hard ones before she managed to grasp
hold of the round, slippery shape without dropping
it. She stared at him blankly as he gave her a
roguish wink and turned back to his work clipping
away busily and whistling as if he hadn't a care in
the world, which she supposed was the case. She
regarded him for a moment or two, with a deep
frown between her brows, and then she whirled
away to stride back into the house to deposit the
glass in the sink. Oddly enough, since she'd been
expecting some kind of criticism from him about
the obvious differences between Ian and herself,
she actually felt let down.

It was a silly reaction to a silly subject. She
shrugged jerkily and resolved to dismiss the whole
thing from her mind. It appeared that Jason was
learning that he had no say about whom she dated
after all.

She had to work that evening, and after

spending the afternoon reading in the shade, she went inside to shower and change into her work clothes. The uniform that the waitresses were supposed to wear was not strict; they had matching blouses which they could wear with any dark skirt of their choice, along with stylish, yet comfortable shoes. Once at work, she would don a pretty, yet serviceable apron, in which she could hold her tips, a handful of handy match books, and her pad and pen. Since today was Sunday, the restaurant closed two hours early, and so she could look forward to being home at a decent time tonight.

She searched for her father, kissed him good night, and then headed to the double garage to climb into her Volvo. A quickly depressed control button and a moment's patient waiting had the door humming up silently behind her. Herb had insisted on automatic controls for the garage doors. That way, she needn't step out of her car until she was safely inside, since the garage was connected to the small family-room. Her father was a very heavy sleeper and never awakened when she arrived home late at night.

Robbie backed down the driveway, pausing only to make sure that the door slid down properly after her, before she glanced over to the Morrows' house. Jason was trimming a large bush in the front garden, and she half-lifted her hand as if to wave at him, but he didn't look her way. She let her hand drop to the wheel, then, and backed until she could pull around in the large circle of pavement which was the end of their cul-de-sac. She pulled away.

Unknown to her, Jason straightened from his work and stared after her disappearing car, his light eyes shaded by one long-fingered hand, his face inscrutable.

Work started well enough. She waited on a family of five as soon as she arrived, and they were particularly nice, leaving her a substantial tip. Then she had a series of couples, as most of the tables in the station allotted to her were for two. The cooks were in rare form, without a single squabble amongst them the entire evening. Usually they fought like squawking chickens, their regulation white hats bobbing and weaving emphatically. The night manager, a handsome, distinguished-looking man, disappeared as was his habit when things were going well. When she carried out one couple's meal, she found that her once-vacant larger table had been filled with several chattering young women. The hostess had set them up with water glasses and menus, and so after serving the couple with their order, she stopped to talk pleasantly for a moment or two with the group. The women appeared to be in fine spirits, which lent itself to a good experience for all concerned, and as Robbie excused herself and made her way towards the back again, she found that Ian had been quietly seated at one of the empty tables for two.

A smile of pleasure lit her face and she bid him a quiet greeting as she passed his table with the promise of coming back soon to take his order. He let his face crease into a lovely, welcoming smile for her and told her he was in no hurry, as he sent a quick look over to her large table.

After she had taken the women's orders, all separate tickets, of course, she sped to the back to put the tickets up, stopped at the bar to pick up their drinks and then served them with a quick word and a smile. She hurried over to Ian, laughing and exaggeratedly breathless.

'I thought you were going to be leaving,' she said, smiling down at his dark, handsome countenance.

His smile, accompanied by the warm, sparkling look in his eyes made her feel very good indeed. 'I leave tomorrow,' he said, closing the menu and setting it aside. 'So I thought I would come and see you before I went.'

She nodded, pleased with the words whether he'd meant them or not. 'Well, I'm glad you did,' she told him. She gestured quickly to the menu. 'Have you decided what you'd like?'

'No, I haven't,' he said, leaning his elbows on the table and looking up at her, dark head tilted. 'Just give me the usual, I suppose.' She nodded again and jotted down the name of his favourite seafood dish, along with his normal drink. Ian was very much a creature of habit. 'Are you busy this weekend?' he asked.

'I work Saturday since I had time off last night, but I'm off Sunday,' she said, her head bent, brown hair gleaming shiny and smooth in the muted lighting. She looked up unexpectedly from under her brows, and found him casting an appreciative eye at the young women at her large table, which made her grin. She was under no illusions about Ian, for all that she liked him. He was definitely one to cast his net far and wide.

He turned his attention back to her, realised that he had been caught, and grinned unashamedly. 'Shall we plan to do something on Sunday, then?' he asked her. 'I can call later on in the week for more definite plans, if you would like.'

'That'll be fine,' she assured him, eyes twinkling. Then she excused herself, checked on her other tables, and went to the back to see if any of her orders were nearing completion.

Slightly later, while she was taking a quick break and talking briefly to another waitress, a likeable woman and one of her favourite co-workers, she happened to look up to her right. Across the restaurant, just being seated, was Jason along with an incredibly beautiful brunette. Robbie stopped short and stared. It was not all that unusual, for nearly everyone in the restaurant was turning to look at the tall, slim couple as they took their seats. Jason looked distinguished and remote in his well-fitting, elegant dark suit while the woman was a perfect foil for him, being raven-haired and wearing a very simple, very lovely crimson dress, which seemed to shimmer slightly in the light, calling attention to the slim, yet lush curves of her white-limbed body.

Robbie couldn't say whom she stared at most, the woman for being so outstandingly lovely, or Jason, for having been the one who was escorting her. Her conception of him was, almost unconsciously, taking a gigantic shift in perspective. She shook herself free of the fascination the couple held for her and then glanced over to Ian. The curve of her lips twisted and became wry, since he was staring at the couple as much as anyone in the place, his coffee-cup halfway to his mouth, the look in his dark eyes frankly stunned. She had seen that look before in other men's eyes. She knew what it meant.

As she went back to work, she checked her wrist-watch and estimated fifteen minutes. It took Ian exactly seven. He left his meal unfinished, which told her that she had badly underestimated his reaction to the unknown woman, and soon he was over at their table, talking smoothly. Jason's reaction was to sit back slowly and smile, amusement obvious on his lean, tanned features even from where she was. The women at her large table heaved a collective sigh of disappointment, for though many of them were attractive, none could hold a candle to the brunette, and they knew it.

Robbie checked Ian's table quietly and found his bill gone, along with a generous tip tucked under the rim of his plate, and so she discreetly signalled for a waiter to come and clear the table.

As for herself, she kept well away from Jason and his date. Jason might not even be aware that she was working tonight, as he hadn't seen her leave the house. She had no wish to intrude on their evening any more than Ian had already. He was still with them, laughing at something the striking brunette had said, his smile devilish and eye-catching, his eyes brilliant and black.

A little later, as she swept away from one of her newer tables, order pad clutched in her hand as she headed for the back, she happened to glance over to Jason and his woman-friend, which she seemed to do rather frequently, and she found

Jason's eyes on her. She smiled quickly at him and waved in all friendliness. His hand lifted briefly in response, but she didn't go over even then. She had too much work to do.

Though the first part of the evening had gone quite quickly, the latter part seemed to drag on interminably. The customers slowed down and she had fewer tables towards the end, which was the general trend on Sundays. As a consequence, she had a great deal of her clean-up work completed by the time the restaurant doors were locked for the night. She was slipping out earlier than most of the others as the time neared eleven and she was home well before midnight.

She pulled quietly into the driveway at home, and as she waited for the garage door to open, she glanced over to the Morrows' house. It was dark, with no sign of life at all. With lightning suddenness, the thought came to her that perhaps Jason wasn't home yet, which led her to wonder where he would be, and if he would be home before the night was out.

With very careful hands, she drew into the garage and switched off her engine, listening as the door hummed down behind her, sitting quietly in the dark shadows without moving. She didn't know why, but she was oddly shocked. She had never considered the subject before, but to all intents, Jason was a perfectly normal male, and the woman he had been with was particularly ravishing. It would have been quite understandable if he didn't show at all before morning. Certainly he was a strikingly handsome man in his own right, a fact which she'd only lately begun to appreciate.

A flashing image came to her mind, and once entered, she couldn't dispel it. Jason, bending his light brown, well-shaped head slowly down to waiting, lush lips, which fastened eagerly, hotly on to his. The crimson and ivory body melting against his hard, masculine body. The woman's raven hair falling over his dark, encircling arm. His broad shoulders bowed over her, her slim arms languidly entwining his bent neck, her hands stroking his sleek hair. His hands caressing her body, taking off the crimson dress, marking the delicate skin.

Robbie's face flushed abruptly in a hot tide of red blood, and her hands clenched spasmodically, bone-white on the steering wheel in front of her. A muscle ticked in the sleek line of her jaw, and she felt as though she had been burned by the images that came, unbidden, to her inner eye. It was because she was intensely embarrassed. She would have felt the same if she had conjured up such thoughts about her father and his attractive widow. She would have felt the same had she a brother and considered his sexuality.

She rocketed out of her car and rushed through the garage and house to prepare feverishly for bed. What an awful thing to think about. Jason's sexual encounters were his affair, and none of her business. But then came the question, blurting uncontrollably into her mind, and she began to wonder just how many women Jason might already have known.

In bed, she buried her head deep under her pillows, though it was dark and there was no one to see her anyway. Her long legs twisted in the cool bed-sheets. A night breeze wafted through the open window, lazily stirring her curtains. She twisted on to her back and stared sightlessly up at the dark ceiling, unable to halt her teeming, weltering confusion of thoughts.

She had never experimented sexually, though she knew many girls and women who had. Affairs at work were multitudinous and commonplace. Some of the waitresses fell into bed with any man who had money and looks, especially money. Robbie was no naïve little girl; she knew and understood quite well the sometimes torturous paths romantic involvements could take. But along with her femininity, sexual interest had come late into her life, and she had never been in the position when the time or the mood had seemed right. A few of her boyfriends had pressured her, and even Ian had shown a willingness to take their relationship a bit further than she would have liked, but she could never muster enough enthusiasm or foolishness for that first, awesome plunge. She had been physically stirred, sure, but not rocked to her foundations, pleasantly aroused but not shattered by the strength of her own passion. The scenes her imagination had now brought to life were raw, powerful, surging, and she curled her body tight in confused reaction.

She didn't know. Perhaps she was indeed a naïve little fool. Her mind and body certainly burned with mortification. Her breath came short and shallow, and her muscles were tense. Surely, it was mortification.

She tossed and turned for the entire night, and as a consequence, she rose heavy-eyed and irritable the next morning at eight. She was tired at the beginning of the day and she had to work until late that evening. It did not seem to be the best of starts to her week. Her room was quite cool, almost uncomfortably so, and a quick look outside informed her that the day was overcast and windy. She slammed her window shut, resisting with all her might the urge to race downstairs and see if Jason's car was in the Morrows' driveway. He would be leaving soon for work, as would her father.

With her dressing gown thrown carelessly over her slim shoulders, still wearing her thigh-length nightshirt and with bare legs flashing, she went down the stairs to find her father. Herb was sipping coffee at the dining-table, ready for work in his sober business suit and tie, greying hair neat and glistening from his morning shower. He looked quite surprised to see her so early.

'And a good morning to you, I think,' he said in reply to her mumbled greeting. She could feel him watching as she made her way to the counter and carelessly sloshed hot coffee into a large, hand-painted mug. She went to the table and plopped down into a chair to stare into space moodily. 'Rather early for you to be up, isn't it?'

'I couldn't get to sleep last night,' she said and yawned into her hand. 'I think I must have gone to bed too early.'

'Hadn't expected to see you today, since you work tonight,' grunted her father. She had to leave before he got home, so at times they didn't see each other for days. They had a habit of leaving notes for each other, and slips of white paper were periodically scattered throughout the house.

A quick hard knock sounded at the nearby sliding glass doors, and Robbie jumped where she sat, while Herb rose to answer it. She bowed her tousled head and leaned her chin into one hand as behind her Jason's voice answered cheerfully. 'I came by to borrow a cup of milk for my coffee, if you've got it. I ran out yesterday and forgot to pick up more before everything closed.'

'We don't want it back when you're done with it,' said Robbie sourly as she lifted her head; to which her father laughed.

There was a sliding swish as Herb pushed the doors open wider. 'Come on in, Jason. You're welcome to have coffee here, unless you've already made some for yourself?'

'No, as a matter of fact, I haven't. Thank you,' Jason replied. 'Sit back down, Herb, I'll get it. Good grief, man, don't stand on ceremony with me! Why, good morning, Rob. You look like the devil.'

She turned her head, to eye his crisp figure evilly. 'You'd better be careful, or I might tell you where to go,' she threatened, bringing an unrepentant grin to his face while her father admonished her mildly.

Jason was also ready for work, dressed in a light blue summer suit, his brown hair dampened by his shower, looking even darker, his light grey eyes startling. He brought his cup over to the table and sat, talking desultorily with Herb for a few minutes while she remained silent, until her father finally rose to leave.

'I'd better get going before I'm late for the office,' he grunted. 'I have a longer drive ahead of me than you.' He bent to press a quick kiss to

Robbie's upturned cheek. 'I'll see you tomorrow, honey. Have a good day.'

''Bye, Dad,' she said and watched from under heavy lids as he walked out of the kitchen. Silence settled like old dust over them as they listened to her father's departure. After a moment, the adjoining door to the garage opened and closed, and they heard the far-off sounds of Herb starting his car and the garage door whining up.

Robbie bent her head and pressed her fingers to her temples, squeezing her eyes closed tightly in an effort to shake herself alert. She avoided looking in Jason's direction as he sat just to her right, around the corner of the table. The images of last night came to mind, and she shifted uneasily in her seat.

The silence continued until she began to realise how heavy and unusual it was. Jason wasn't even stirring in his chair or drinking his coffee. She opened her eyes and turned her head to look at him, finding that he was regarding her sharply, intently, with a frown lowering his brows. Under the curious weight of his own light-coloured gaze, her own brown eyes widened, puzzled.

'You okay, Rob?' Jason asked finally, his voice very quiet in the empty house, even diffident.

Surprise showed in her expression. She cupped her coffee mug between her hands and hunched her shoulders, shifting to look down at the glossy finish of the table surface. 'Sure, why?' she muttered and, to her frustration, felt a betraying wave of heat course up her neck. She could only hope that with her dark tan, it wasn't particularly visible.

'You look so tired,' he said, leaning forward. Unconsciously, she shrank back slightly. His eyes were everywhere, on her silken, tousled hair, on her downbent eyes, on the circles beneath them, on her slim, restless hands. Without looking up again, she thought of how fresh and alert he looked, but then he had always been thus even after just a few hours of rest. Then she winced, involuntarily, at where that led her. 'What's wrong?'

'Nothing!' she exclaimed and thrust out of her chair to stride for the coffee pot. 'Do you want any more coffee?' she threw over her shoulder.

His reply seemed slow in coming. 'No, thanks.' She poured hers quickly, experience making her judge accurately to a drop, and then she returned to her seat. Jason was leaning back now, his face turned to her, his vivid eyes running over every plane and curve of her expression. As she took her seat again, wondering when he would be leaving, he said, voice sudden in the stillness, 'I'm . . . very sorry about last night.'

Her dark eyes flashed to his face. 'What the hell does that mean?' she asked, with a blink.

His own eyes were relentless. She wondered briefly what he saw with those eyes. 'I didn't know that Walsh would be there to see you, otherwise I would have taken Linda somewhere else.'

'What?' She was astounded. 'How would you have known, and why on earth would you have gone somewhere else?'

His head turned away sharply, and he closed his eyes to rub them with thumb and forefinger. 'I'm not saying this well at all. Look, I just wanted to say that I'm sorry that last night happened, that

Walsh was so damned obvious. I would have expected better from him.'

Robbie narrowed her eyes, cat-like. 'Just what do you mean by that? You think I'm jealous over Ian or something?'

His eyes snapped back to her face, quick, flashing. 'Aren't you?' he queried softly.

'No!' she said, perhaps too violently. 'Of course not. That's just how Ian is. I would have been surprised if he hadn't gone over to your table; that woman was so lovely.'

Jason's surprise was swift in running over his features. 'But doesn't that bother you?' She looked and felt strange, as she thought that one over in silence. Then she opened her mouth, only to close it again without replying, for perhaps she should be bothered, but she wasn't, she wasn't at all. What she was bothered about was so ridiculous, and so obviously none of her business, that she was at a loss as to how to respond to his question.

Jason's rather stern expression gentled, and he reached out with his hand to cover her forearm. His touch was electric to her, and she jumped at the sensation, wondering involuntarily what and where he had touched with those square, well-tended hands. 'Rob, stop seeing him,' he urged softly. She stared at him, even more astonished, her large eyes quite blank. Jason searched them, and then he took a quick breath. 'Can't you see that he's no good for you? You'll only hurt yourself needlessly if you see him anymore. He's unreliable, as slippery and as treacherous as a snake.'

'I . . . always did like snakes,' she said then,

irrelevantly. She stared down at her cup and abruptly raised it to drink from the warm, steaming liquid within. His hand fell away. 'I mean, they're such lovely, graceful creatures really, though certainly not cuddly like a pet. The way they can shed their old skin and emerge looking new and jewel-like is simply amazing...'

Jason moved convulsively and muttered something under his breath that sounded like, 'Damn!' Then, louder, with audible restraint, he told her stiltedly, 'Rob, I just don't want to see you hurt.'

She turned her eyes to him. 'I'm not going to be hurt,' was her attempted reassurance, as she felt very touched by his concern.

But his response was explosive. 'Not going to be hurt!' he snapped, looking suddenly angry, his eyes sparkling hard and bright. 'What are you now, for God's sake? Look at you, you've got shadows under your eyes, you're pale, you're exhausted! Why couldn't you sleep last night? What was on your mind?'

'I ...' Her eyes widened, stricken, for she couldn't think of a single excuse to give him. Her mind was a blank, and she certainly couldn't tell the truth.

He didn't merely look angry. For some odd reason, he looked furious. 'See?' he sneered. 'Haven't anything to say, have you? Admit the truth, Robbie! You're in too deep!'

'You haven't any idea what you're talking about,' she told him, coldly, through a confusion of anger and bewilderment. How odd he was. How wrong.

'Elaborate.' The word was succinct. 'Wasn't that

why you refused to come over to our table last
night to say hello?'

'I was leaving you to some privacy!' she cried
out impatiently, and pushed out of her chair to put
her back to him in exasperation.

'I don't believe you anymore, why can't you tell
me the truth?'

'I have no intention of telling you a damned
thing!' Couldn't, wouldn't, God, what she couldn't
tell him.

Silence hit them like something crushing. She
turned to face him and found his eyes peculiarly
stark. 'You used to tell me everything,' he
whispered through thinned lips.

And suddenly she could sense and see the hurt
she had unwittingly caused him, and it was
throbbing through his entire, tense body. 'God,'
she choked and put her hand to her forehead in
distress, in remorse. Then she hurt, too, and she
said jerkily, 'I didn't mean it that way, Jason.'

'The hell you didn't,' he said thinly.

'Things are different between us, now!' she
cried. And then the pain was unexpectedly, sharply
raw and welling up in her, along with the
loneliness she'd felt when he had left. 'You went
away! There are six years between what we were,
and what we are! We're not the same, and we can't
be good old pals anymore! It's gone.'

Then suddenly he was standing, and she
couldn't remember seeing him move. He strode
over to her with quick, violent movements. His
hands snaked out and twined themselves into the
hair at the back of her head. He jerked her close
and stared down, eyes molten, into her face. She

was in a state of shock. Never had he handled her this way. Never had he shown such emotion. 'You're going to break yourself over him,' he bit out between twisted lips. He gave her a little shake. 'You're being a fool over him. Can't you see what he is? Damn you! You're going to break your silly little heart.'

Then before she could move, or speak, or even breathe, he released her, spun on his heel, and was gone.

CHAPTER THREE

Work that evening was as exhausting as she had known it would be. She dragged, her eyes heavy, her arms feeling leaden. Each laden tray was an effort to lift to her shoulder, and she nearly dropped several orders. When she finally slunk into the garage and turned off her car, she didn't even move for long moments. Her neck hurt, her back ached, the muscles in her legs throbbed. She wasn't good at functioning on little sleep. She was the kind of person who needed a set schedule, or she lost all her vitality.

No. Her head sagged, and then she forced her body to climb out of the car. The door slammed, loud in the confined darkness. It wasn't lack of sleep that bothered her. She could do as well as the next person on an occasional short night's rest. What lowered her spirits was the memory of that morning and her painful encounter with Jason. She hadn't realised how much she had missed his companionship, hadn't realised that she would reveal it so starkly and so completely in her tone and words, to either him or herself.

Somehow the hurt had only surfaced when she had well and truly acknowledged that their past relationship was gone. People grew up, moved away, pursued different lifestyles. But the tears pricked at her eyes as she moved clumsily through the darkened house. She didn't want to let go of the past. The past was happiness to her. She wasn't happy now, and it was a bitter admission to make. She was lonely. She existed well enough, as her father had existed for years now, but she wasn't happy.

Sleep was a gradual darkening of her depression, a gentle easing away of thought and sight and sense until she awakened the next morning, rested but not refreshed. Robbie dawdled through her morning shower, dressed in her brief, black bikini with a white pair of shorts pulled over her hips, and after a ritual glass of orange juice and some light cleaning, she went outside to lie in the sun and read.

She had nothing to do for the next two days except to catch up on her house-cleaning and amuse herself in any way she wished. The next evening she was scheduled to work was Thursday. Robbie situated the lounge chair so that she caught full advantage of the sun, and then after liberally coating her already dark body with lotion, which she now used to stop her skin drying out rather than for tanning purposes, she settled on her stomach and opened her book.

Soon she was quite engrossed in the story. The book was entitled *Burn Out*, written by a woman named Devan Forrester, and was supposed to be at least partially autobiographical. It had been on the bestseller list for ten months and was nominated for several literary awards. The story was tense, dark, filled with anguish and also filled with a powerful strength and hope. There were strong contrasts of light and dark in the plot, and a universal theme of revitalisation that caught at Robbie's flagging spirits and quickened her heart.

Revitalisation, low ebb and high tide, great strengths and terrible frailty. This was the stuff of human life. Her book lowered slowly, until it rested on the chair and she was staring sightlessly at the sunny scene before her. The word kept echoing queerly in her mind, with a heavy emphasis. Revitalisation. Odd, how depression could mar one's outlook with tunnel vision, until all one could see and sense and taste was the darkness. Her optimism reasserted itself, and though she still mourned the scene with Jason yesterday, she now had hopes of patching the tattered, neglected fabric of their relationship together, perhaps continuing with something new.

Later that afternoon, her empty stomach finally made itself known in no uncertain terms, making her leave the lounge chair and head back inside for a quick, light snack. Since it was nearly time for her father to return home, she limited herself to an apple and a granola bar, while thinking ahead to what she should make for supper.

She and Herb fluctuated with the chores, though more often than not she was the one who cooked their evening meals. Herb did the grocery shopping and took the rubbish out, and as they owned a dishwasher, they both took responsibility for loading and unloading it.

She wasn't exactly enthusiastic about working over a hot stove, and so she resolved to make a fancy salad, with delicately flavoured chicken sandwiches, using the cold meat left over in the refrigerator. That decision made, she headed for the stairs, intending to shower and change out of her swimsuit.

As she reached the hallway, however, the doorbell rang, and so she changed course in midstride to answer the summons. When she pulled the door open, she found Jason leaning casually against the doorpost, his light brown hair ruffled. He was dressed in dark suit slacks, and had apparently stopped by after coming straight home from the office, though he had taken the time to rid himself of his tie and jacket. His white shirt was open halfway down his chest with the sleeves rolled up in the heat.

For just a split second, she had full view of his profile as he looked over the lawn, that young, lean face, the weariness in his eyes that was more an expression than physical manifestation, the firmness of his sensual mouth. Then he turned his head and smiled faintly into her closed, wary eyes.

'May I come in?'

She started and came to herself, and then backed away wordlessly so that he could enter the hall. He ran his vivid gaze down her body. The bikini was basically a series of small triangles in strategic places, leaving on open view her narrow rib-cage, the graceful swelling of hip-bones under an even narrower waist, and long, lean, lovely legs. She was in good physical condition from the demands of her job, her muscles tight, flowing, her skin very dark and shiny with lotion.

Under his gaze, she lifted one slim hand and pushed her smooth brown hair back. It fell straight to her shoulders from her strong, yet refined features. Somewhere along the line, her face had sharpened from the round immaturity of a child. Her brown eyes searched his, questioningly. He seemed fascinated by something in her.

When he didn't say anything straight away, she asked, 'Would you like something cold to drink?'

'Please,' he responded immediately. When she turned to go back to the kitchen, he followed close behind, and after she had poured two glasses of tea and handed one to him, he leaned against the counter. One hand was propped back on the counter's edge, while with the other, he swirled his glass and stared down into the clear, brown depths. Light was reflected from the ice cubes and liquid in brilliant splashes of honey. Robbie kept her gaze on his glass while half-heartedly sipping from her own.

'Did you have a good day at work?' she ventured at last.

'Mmm, yes,' he replied, absently enough, and then frowned. 'Rob, about yesterday morning . . .'

She moved involuntarily, jerkily, and put her back to him. She could feel his eyes on her, running down the sleek, slender lines of her silken brown back. She wondered where her usual grace had gone. 'Please,' she interrupted quickly, at his slight pause. 'Do we have to talk about it?'

'I was hurt, yesterday,' he said with difficulty. It brought her back to face him.

Her brown eyes glittered bright and wet. 'I'm sorry. I didn't mean to hurt you,' she told him, unsteadily. It seemed as if a gulf separated them, not just the tiled expanse of the kitchen floor. She couldn't distinguish his features, his lean, long body a blur through her tears.

'It wasn't necessarily that you hurt me, Rob,' he

whispered. For a person whom she had always
considered to be a strong individual, he was
showing an astonishing vulnerability. 'It was just
that I hurt.'

'Me, too,' she muttered and hung her head
dejectedly. To her intense chagrin, she felt her lips
beginning to quiver, and quick hot tears spilled
down her cheeks, two streaking paths. Her hair
swung forward, but not quickly enough. From
where she was, she could hear his indrawn breath.

His mellow voice sounded strained then, as he
told her, 'What you said yesterday needn't be true,
Rob. I know we've changed. But I value what we
had. You were my best friend.'

She put her hand to her forehead, blinking
rapidly. Strange, how she never cried when she
argued with anyone else. Not with her father, not
with her girlfriends, nor with the restaurant manager. Only Jason brought that out. Her own voice a
bare thread of sound, she whispered, 'I missed you
when you left. I didn't have anyone to talk to.'

'I love you,' he said.

Her heart gave a great, half-frightened leap. Her
head snapped up, and her brown eyes blazed.

He didn't see. His own gaze was directed at the
floor at his feet. 'I can't say that to many people,
certaintly not to any of my male friends. It's just
not something you communicate that often, know
what I mean? But I do, Rob. I want us to continue
being friends very much. Maybe we can't have
quite the openness we had before. Maybe we can,
but we have to try.'

She was utterly stunned. He meant that he
loved her as a friend. How else would he have

meant it? Of course he had only meant friendship, but when he had said the words, everything inside her had gone crazy. Slowly sanity began to rein in her teeming thoughts; slowly she gained control over herself and realised the value of what he had just offered her.

This was a man in the first flush of his maturity. This was a man who refused to view an open declaration of feelings as being unmasculine. This was a man with integrity, constant values, high goals. This was a man with a golden future ahead of him, his personality more than fulfilling a potential that she had scarcely realised as a child. This was a rare, special individual, and she would be eager to accept any friendship at all with him.

His grey eyes lifted to her face. She smiled at him. 'I love you too, Jason,' she said quietly, friend to friend, adult to adult. And somewhere in that smile, she let go of her yearnings for their childhood, accepting the changes in herself and in him.

His answering smile lit his entire, lean face with pleasure. He set his glass down. 'Come here, you,' he said, and opened his arms to her.

She laughed and regardless of the slippery lotion all over her body or his business clothes, she walked over to him. His strong arms folded around her, his head bent over hers, and he held her tight against his chest. She could feel the warm skin of his forearms against her bare back, the slight rasp of his cheek against hers, his legs long, lean, harder than her own, and she sighed as her arms wrapped around his neck. 'You're going to have lotion all over your clothes,' she told him, to which he laughed also.

'I don't care. As dirty as you and I have been on occasion, this is nothing.' His hands were at her naked back, and she felt his fingers slip down her ribs to her waist. Something tightened in her, an unfathomable response. She leaned back as he lifted his head, and she realised that he, too, was tense for some reason.

His light grey eyes flickered. Her own large brown orbs were plainly bewildered. He bent his head and pressed his well-shaped lips against hers briefly. It was a light kiss, full of affection and practically nothing else. She couldn't think why a shiver ran down her spine, to weaken the backs of her knees. He was firm and controlled, very controlled, as he lifted his head and smiled easily down into her eyes. His arms loosened casually and she stepped back. Then he half-turned to take up his tea again, so easy, so utterly natural.

But when she turned back for her own glass, she was shaking, in a state of incomprehension, wondering what had been touched to life inside her at the feel of those cool, masculine lips. Wondering what he had felt, and why the tiny, betraying muscle in his jaw was ticking spasmodically under that calm façade.

She drank her tea and then winced. She'd taken far too big a gulp, and it hurt all the way down, exploding coolly into her stomach. 'Would you like to come back over for supper, after you've changed?' she threw over her shoulder. Then she turned to look at him, trying to read his expression. There was nothing unusual in his countenance. 'It isn't much,' she felt bound to continue. 'Just salad and sandwiches.'

'Anything would be great, if I didn't have to make it,' he told her drily. Startled, she threw back her head and laughed at him. 'Yes, I would, thanks. When should I be back? Will I have time for a quick shower?'

'Sure, we can start whenever you get over here. I have to take one, too, anyway,' she assured him.

With that, he left, after putting his glass in the sink. Though she knew she should get moving also, needing not only to shower but to prepare the supper she'd offered him, she didn't stir for several long, thought-filled moments. She was trying to establish just what she had felt during those brief moments when Jason had held her. It was a great pity that she could come to no real conclusion.

When Robbie finally ducked into the shower cubicle, she had been indoors long enough to have cooled sufficiently to prevent her being unduly shocked by using lukewarm water. She washed her hair quickly and afterwards put it into a towelled turban while she dressed in a sleeveless white blouse with cherry-red dress shorts. The vibrancy of the colours brought out her tan nicely, attractive hues for the browns in her hair and eyes. Then she emphasised her facial features with make-up, though why she bothered when she was only going to be with Jason and her father, she didn't know. Only then did she let her hair fall, already partially dry, and after brushing it vigorously so that it fell in soft bouncy waves to her shoulders, she ran down the stairs again, barefoot, and briskly set to work.

Herb had come home while she had been busy

dressing in her room, and he had rapped on her door lightly to let her know of his arrival. He was soon downstairs in a casual change of clothes and looked over her shoulder enquiringly. 'I'm starved,' he said, giving her a pat for a greeting. 'Is there anything I can do?'

'Yes, why don't you set the table?' she told him, shifting her foot away as the toe of his shoe had caught her on the heel. 'Jason's coming over, so there'll be three of us.'

Soon everything was ready, the chicken sandwiches made and nicely arranged on a central serving platter, with the lush, crispy salad nearby, drinks poured, and dressings set handily on the table. Jason rapped on the sliding glass door, and Herb let him in, while Robbie peered into the freezer to see if they still had any ice-cream. The half-gallon box, present just the day before, was gone.

'Good grief!' she exclaimed in astonishment, as she slammed the small upper door closed. She turned to stare at her father, while Jason, unknown to her, eyed her legs with a somewhat secretive smile. 'Have you eaten that entire box already?'

Herb looked sheepish. He was a tolerant man when it came to food and could eat with equanimity just about any dish she made, good or bad, but his two abiding passions were beer and ice-cream. He could polish off a gallon box within a few days, though he was a bit more strict with his love for beer. He kept his figure trim only by vigorous walking during the week and long golf sessions on the weekends.

Robbie relented and flashed a quick smile to
Jason, who was now clad in jeans and a short-
sleeved, rugby-style shirt which matched the grey
of his eyes. Her gaze bounced off his masculine
figure self-consciously, as she mused that lately
whenever she saw him, the solidity of his body
struck her anew.

As the meal was already set out, they were
sitting down to eat quickly enough, and while
Robbie concentrated on listening and eating, the
other two fell into a discussion about work.

'Well, it certainly looks as though you're doing
extremely well for yourself, my boy,' said Herb at
last, as he leaned back and prepared to nurse his
drink idly, his plate neatly clean. He repeated
sagely. 'Extremely well for yourself.'

Jason shrugged, broad shoulders rolling under
his shirt. Robbie knew what those shoulders
looked like, naked. Unseen by either man, her
cheeks suddenly reddened vividly. She studied the
scene outside the glass doors intently until the
flush died away. 'I've got a long way to go, yet,'
Jason was saying easily.

'Mark my words, son. Some men get by, while
others stand out,' her father told him, nodding at
his own observation. Robbie almost smiled until
she looked over to Jason and saw his serious,
polite attentiveness. 'Me, now, I just get by. Very
well, though, I might add. This house is paid for,
and my retirement is taken care of, but I just get
by. You have what it takes to stand out.'

She agreed silently, but Jason was shaking his
head with a slight frown. 'I don't know, Herb.
What you are seeing in me right now might only

be my youth and the energy that comes with it. I've been lucky so far, I haven't had any accidents, haven't had anything go wrong at all. But many potentially great people have something go wrong in their lives.'

He glanced at Robbie sitting quietly at her end of the table, and the look was nearly a caress. It warmed her to a tingling all over. She couldn't remember how she used to feel about him anymore, but if she had felt this good by his positive regard, then it wasn't surprising that she had missed it.

'Yes, but that shouldn't keep one from trying,' her father was saying.

'No, of course not. But as someone has been teaching me lately, I find that if I can live just being the man I want to be, then I will be content with my life. As for any material or worldly success, I'll accept what comes my way.'

'Sounds like you know a wise person,' commented Herb with a smile.

Jason grinned quickly and flicked Robbie a sideways, laughing glance. 'You should know, since you've been living with her for the past twenty-two years.'

'Oh, yeah?' Her father looked at her in somewhat pleased appraisal, while she blinked several times rapidly.

'What are you talking about, I've never said any such thing to you!' she exclaimed with some heat, as she stood and began to clear away the dishes energetically.

Jason rose to help. 'Sure you have. You just haven't put it into those exact words,' he replied quietly. She felt odd, surprised, taken aback. 'I went to college, and immediately got wrapped up in my career goals, the competition, grade point averages, yearly incomes. I got ambitious, Rob, and I studied hard for four years to get a good start on my working life. Then I came back here, plunged into the rat race, and found you, living serenely and taking your own sweet time about deciding what to do with yourself. It brought me back down to earth again, and showed me the things that really do matter.'

She scowled fiercely, as she carried a load of dishes to the waiting machine. Neither of them realised when Herb quietly slipped away to find his evening newspaper. 'Don't make me out to be some kind of paragon,' she said, ostensibly irritable. 'I don't need that kind of pressure on me.'

'I'm not making you out to be a paragon,' he said quietly, putting his own handful down on the counter. He leaned his elbows on it, back curved, head turned to her as she squatted on her heels to stack things into the dishwasher. When she glanced up, she saw how the slanting evening sun lit the back of his head to gold and brown, while in shadow, his eyes gleamed palely. 'What you're doing isn't even profound, though at times it can be. What you're doing, Rob, is being sane while the world rushes crazily around you. You've taught me something, sweetheart. When I find myself going too fast, all I need to do is slow down.'

She ducked her head, and her hair, now quite dry, swung against her cheeks. 'Sometimes I think

I should have done differently,' she confessed quietly. 'Here I am, twenty-two years old, I don't know what I want in my near future, I don't know where to go from here. Do you know, the people who went to college from my senior class have already graduated? Maybe I'm wrong. Maybe I should have been one of them, too.'

'You shouldn't have been if you didn't want to be in college,' he replied, touching at her hair and tucking it behind her ear. With a great effort she managed not to flinch away in surprise. 'Above all else, you should do what you want to do. Now, who was it who told me that?'

Despite herself, she began to smile. 'I need somewhere to go from here,' she sighed. 'I need some kind of goal.'

'Why don't you take some classes?' he suggested, shifting his weight from one leg to another. 'You were always excellent in maths, weren't you? And what of those drafting courses you took in high school?'

'I thought about studying to become an architect once,' she told him dreamily, her fingers curving gently around the door of the dishwasher. She had finished stacking dishes for several minutes now and had only just realised it.

'Why don't you?' he asked softly, his eyes running over her face time and time again.

Her expression abruptly closed, her eyes flashing downward, and she shut the machine door, then started the cycle. She stepped towards the sink quickly, wetted the dish-cloth and went to the dining table to wipe it energetically.

'Rob. Roberta.' Her swiping motions stilled

completely, and she turned her head to one side. Had she ever heard him call her anything but Rob before this? She doubted it. 'Please don't run away from this.' She didn't move. 'I'm not pressuring you.' That last was said with some defensiveness.

It softened her into turning back around to face him. She could hear what he was asking. He was asking her to confide in him, the way she used to. She put out her tongue, moistened her lips nervously, and found it easy to say after all. 'I'm scared. I've never been to college. It's been years since I've studied. I've fallen out of the habit. Maybe I wouldn't do well, maybe I'm too old . . .'

'Good God!' he expostulated. 'That's the worst excuse I've ever heard you give about anything, and let me tell you, I've heard some bad ones.' Her expression was briefly sticken, and she bowed her head, abashed. He thrust away from the counter, which he had been leaning against after turning to watch her movements. Three quick, easy strides brought him right beside her, and he said gently, 'I understand being scared, Rob. But you shouldn't let it cripple you.'

Her forehead wrinkled in distress. It sounded easy from him, when his university days were behind him. 'What if I didn't do well?' she asked in a burst of uncertainty.

'You're not alone in the world, you know,' said Jason wryly. Then as she stared at him, he offered with studied nonchalance, 'I could always help you study.'

Her astonishment showed plainly in her face. 'You wouldn't want to do that,' she replied, in immediate rejection. Then, 'Would you?'

He was gazing at her patiently, amusedly, affectionately. 'Have you ever known me to offer something when I didn't mean it?' he retorted laughingly, and she shook her head. 'Well, then, what do you think?'

'I think,' she said slowly, with some wickedness through her appreciation, 'that it's one of the nicest propositions I've had in a long time.'

He winced at that. 'I don't think I'll pry into that statement. Just think about it,' he advised. 'Don't close doors on yourself needlessly, do you hear?'

She threaded her arm through his to squeeze it against her side briefly. His brows rose quizzically as he looked down at her, though his eyes were warm and smiling. 'You're very good to me,' she told him quietly.

His face subtly lit with pleasure. 'What else are friends for?' he replied lightly. She smiled as she withdrew to finish wiping the table, and then she carried the cloth to the sink to rinse it and spread it out to dry. She couldn't have said why exactly, but his response left her feeling a bit flat. It was the strangest thing in the world. She should have been feeling great.

She didn't see him for any length of time throughout the rest of the week. As soon as Thursday rolled around, the pace of her days picked up pleasantly so that Sunday arrived quickly and she had nothing to do for the whole day until she had to prepare herself for her date with Ian.

He had called yesterday morning to finalise plans, and they were going to a show, then out for coffee and dessert. It was a film she had already seen, but as it was very good and also quite hilarious, she didn't bother telling him so. It would be fun to see the film again, and she always enjoyed Ian's company.

Since she had worked yesterday, she had waited until today to mow the lawn, and so she straddled the riding mower and started the engine. Soon she was going merrily around and around the lawn, in smaller, and then even smaller squares until she felt dizzy and the front garden looked neatly shorn. Then she went to the back garden, starting at the left and then going towards the Morrows' yard. When she had almost finished, Jason leaped over the fence that separated the gardens and walked casually her way.

She sent him a wild, gleeful look, and with a horrified shriek, she frantically turned the unwieldy mower around and started riding bumpily away. She heard his aggressive roar in response, and soon he had leaped on to the back to seize control of the steering wheel, leaning over her apprehensively crouched figure. At that, she tried cravenly to abandon ship, but he laughingly grabbed hold of her, clasping her against his chest.

'Whoa, careful!' he exclaimed, while turning the mower back to the small plot of grass still uncut. At the feel of his hard chest at her back, with his arm a strong barrier around her waist, she fell quite still, feeling an absurd surge of pleasure. 'There now, finish your job, and I'll wait inside for you.'

'Okay!' she replied, as she leaned her head back briefly against his shoulder. He squeezed her tightly in response and then leaped off gracefully to stride towards their back door.

She completed the job as quickly as she could, anxious to finish so that she could see Jason, and soon the mower was tucked back in its usual place beside her father's dark sedan. She pushed a button located near the door to the family-room, and sent the garage door down before lightly running inside.

On her way, she peeked quickly into the living-room and grinned as she saw Herb still snoring away loudly on the couch. His head was hidden under a sheaf of the Sunday comics. Then she skipped into the kitchen to find Jason finishing a beer. Beside him sat a newly poured glass of lemonade, which she took with thanks, drinking the cold, tart liquid with pleasure.

She then walked to the table to sprawl in a chair, throwing back her arms and arching her back in a lazy stretch. The movement sent her slight, rounded breasts straining against her tank top, and Jason's eyes lingered on her chest, reminding her that she didn't have a bra on. She abruptly drew straight, flushing slightly as she realised her nipples must have been clearly outlined against the thin, sweat-dampened fabric. She asked, ostensibly nonchalant, 'Having a good weekend?'

'Yeah, I hate to see it end,' he replied, strolling over, beer in one hand. He pulled the chair around to sit on it backwards, lean legs straddling the seat. He leaned his forearms against the back, idly shaking his nearly empty can. 'I have a few weeks of holiday coming up after next week, and then a few more at Christmas.'

'Really? That ought to be fun. Have you decided what you're going to do?' She reached for her glass and sipped at it.

He shook his head. 'Nope. I think I'll just take things as they come. How was work last night?'

'Tiring,' she said and then stifled a yawn. One of the waitresses scheduled called in sick, and the others had to share her station between them, as the manager had been unable to reach anyone else at such short notice. They had been frantically busy, and she had felt as though she'd been run off her legs, but she had walked out of the restaurant with a hundred dollars in tips tucked into her purse.

'Got any plans for the rest of the day?' he asked casually.

Her easy manner and open smile vanished slowly, and she stared at him warily before saying, 'I'm going out with Ian.'

At first she thought there was no visible reaction to her reply, but a closer look at Jason had her noting the suddenly rock-hard rigidity of his jawline, the odd angry glitter in his grey eyes, the white-knuckled appearance of his right hand as he clenched the beer can tightly. It began to crumple under her eyes. 'You're a fool,' he said through stiff lips.

For a moment she couldn't speak, and then with anger rising herself, she said, a thread of steel in her voice, 'I'll thank you to keep such comments to yourself.'

'He's called Linda three times throughout the

week, trying to get her to see him,' Jason
continued harshly.

She stared at him for a moment, feeling that
perhaps she had begun to understand a little. 'Did
she go out with him?' she asked finally, her voice
hushed.

'He was out of town, she said, until Friday, but
she went out with him last night,' he bit out and
apparently only then realised what he was doing to
his beer can. He loosened his grip and set the
gnarled cylinder carefully on to the table.

'I'm sorry,' she offered sympathetically. He
must really be hurt. She hadn't realised that he
cared for the brunette so much. A leaden ache
started somewhere in her chest.

He thrust out of his seat violently, strode away,
and then came back. 'Doesn't that mean anything
to you? Can't you see even now that Walsh is just
playing with you?'

'Ian plays with everybody!' she expostulated,
rising to her feet also, in her agitation. 'For God's
sake, it isn't as if he's married to me!' At that,
Jason's head reared back and his nostrils flared.
He stared at her, eyes leaping. 'What in the world
is the matter with you?'

'I don't want to talk about it!' he snapped and
strode out of the open glass doors. For a moment
she just stared at the blank space where he had
been standing. Then she raced to the door to stick
her head out.

'That's convenient!' she shouted furiously to his
retreating back. He didn't respond. She thrust out
her chin and her brown eyes narrowed in grim
determination. She was going to thrash this out

with him once and for all, whether he liked it or not.

She whipped out of the back door and raced after him.

CHAPTER FOUR

WHEN she reached Jason's side, she had to skip to keep up with his long, angry stride. Apparently he had no intention of stopping, nor did he look down at her. He stared straight ahead, his eyes ominously narrowed, his face hard. If it had been anyone else, she would have thought twice about confronting such strangely intense emotion, but this was Jason. She used to wrestle with him in the dirt, and once, when he had teased her too hard, she had hauled off and let fly with her right arm, bloodying his nose.

She hopped around until she was right in front of him, slim legs planted firmly apart, arms akimbo. He stopped short to avoid smacking into her full tilt and glared at her. 'Get out of my way,' he growled and tried to sidestep around her.

She moved into his path again. 'Hold it, mister.' She shook her finger under his nose and gritted, 'I have a bone to pick with you. You seem to have picked up a nasty habit of starting arguments and then walking out on them, but you're not going to get away with that around me, Jason Morrow!'

He blinked, and his expression grew somewhat milder, but she was too angry to notice. He folded his arms across his chest, muscles flexing, and cocked his head quizzically to one side. 'It appears to me that I can do just about anything I damn well please,' he commented then, deliberately infuriating her.

Robbie eyed him up and down as though seriously contemplating doing him bodily injury. 'What the hell has got into you? I can't figure you out. I don't know you anymore!' she exclaimed exasperatedly.

The expression in his grey eyes changed, and his lips took on a sardonic, wry twist. 'No,' he agreed quietly. 'I don't believe you do.'

'I'm sorry your girlfriend went out with Ian,' she said between her teeth. 'I'm sorry that you mind so much, but there's nothing I can do about it. You're just going to have to accept it.'

He began to look thoughtful, as he considered her dark brown, rather flushed countenance. When he spoke next, his tone was actually cautious. 'Do you mind, Rob? You don't seem too upset.'

'Of course I'm upset!' she shouted and then made an effort to calm down. Her anger ebbing somewhat, she poked her finger half-heartedly into his chest. He snatched at her hand and held it, warm fingers curling around hers. 'I'm upset with you, you big jackass,' she mumbled and tried to tug her hand away. 'My God! I've never known such an obtuse man! I've tried and tried to tell you, Ian is just a good friend. The only one who seems to mind him around here is you.'

'I don't have to like the man just because you do, Robbie.' He seemed quite intent on keeping her hand for a while and playing with her fingers. Light colour suffused her cheeks. She grew absurdly flustered with the half-smiling consideration he was giving her slim hand. He appeared to be in sudden good spirits, and she resigned herself to the realisation that she might never grow to understand him.

'That's certainly not surprising, with all the attention he's been giving your girlfriend, but don't take it out on me, do you hear? I won't stand for it.' Her tone of voice was growing more and more absent, as she found herself tangled into a knot of confusion. He cradled her hand against his chest while watching her face, lightly alert. His actions were totally strange to her. Never had he given her such attention. How odd he had become!

'Sorry,' he said then, rather indifferently. 'Last week I got the impression that you were hurt.'

'I told you I wasn't.'

'I know, but every other woman I've known says just the exact opposite of what she's feeling,' he told her, audible amusement in his voice.

She gave a hard yank and snatched her hand free as she snapped irritably, 'That's one of the grossest stereotypes I've ever heard!' Just how many women had he known intimately? Good grief, he was only twenty-four!

'You know what they say to do when the shoe fits.' He was entertained now, which irritated her all the more.

'One thing hasn't changed about you,' she told him peevishly. 'You're still the most exasperating male I've ever met!' He threw back his head and laughed aloud. Growing diffident then, she turned away and showed great interest in the bushes he kept in such good shape. With a restless hand, she plucked at the tiny leaves, feeling quite warm under the direct glare of the blazing sun. She heard Jason shift behind her and then gave in to the curiosity that had been eating away at her ever since seeing the brunette with him Sunday night. 'How long have you been seeing that Linda what's-her-name?' she asked, supremely indifferent.

'A good four years now,' he replied cheerfully. Her back stiffened as she tried to make sense out of that. Then he explained, 'We went to college together. Linda was in many of the same classes that I was, and when the firm that hired me came to the school to interview graduating accountants, she was hired at the same time.'

She nodded her head jerkily. 'I see.' Her fingers plucked more of the leaves, sending them scattering lightly to the grass.

'We're quite close,' he told her, watching her every move with a guarded closeness that, had she seen it, she would have found quite puzzling.

'I see,' she repeated in a low voice. Of course they would be close. They had many similar interests. Linda was a vibrantly beautiful woman. Apparently she had the intelligence that would have earned his respect as a professional. That would be important to him. Feeling very low in spirits suddenly, she put on her bright face determinedly, before turning around to smile at him. 'Well! I suppose I should go inside to get ready for tonight.' He gave her a curious, unexpectedly sweet smile. It prompted her to pat his arm. 'I shouldn't worry about Linda too much if I were you,' she told him quietly. 'Sooner or later, she'll see what a treasure you are.'

With that, she walked quickly back to the house. She forced herself not to glance back, so she couldn't have known that he turned to stare at her until she rounded the back of the house and was out of his sight. But her back burned the whole way.

She was very subdued when Ian picked her up at six-thirty. He also seemed preoccupied, frowning, withdrawn, as they went straight to the cinema. The show started at seven, and soon Robbie had to wipe her streaming eyes while Ian unashamedly slapped his knee and roared. The film ended up turning the mood of their evening around, and so when they went out for dessert afterwards, they were more relaxed and jovial.

She sat back in her seat at the family restaurant while watching him stir his coffee endlessly. His was a more cheerful countenance, but he still wasn't the Ian she knew, and after a few moments, she leaned forward and asked him, 'Ian, what is it? You're acting as though you haven't a friend in the world.'

'Good God, am I that obvious?' His quick, accompanying gaze was contrite and rueful.

She smiled a little. 'I think I know you rather well by now,' was her only response.

'I'm sorry I'm not better company.'

'That's quite all right,' she was quick to reassure him. After contemplating him for a few moments, she took a gamble and commented softly, 'She's very beautiful, isn't she?'

His dark eyes flashed to her face, surprise blazing hot. 'What do you mean?' he asked very fast.

She confessed, letting her own gaze fall to her hands, linked on the table in front of her, 'Jason told me that you went out with Linda last night. I took a guess. She's the one you're thinking of, isn't she?'

For a moment he didn't say anything, but then with some heat he exclaimed, 'Never in my life have I taken out one woman to discuss another! Yes, dammit, and I'm sorry. I just can't get her out of my mind.'

'She seems to have that kind of personality,' Robbie said mildly, though it wasn't exactly Linda's personality that she was thinking of. A sort of resigned sadness settled on her shoulders while she took her cup and sipped at her hot drink. She wondered briefly, without malice, how it would feel to attract all sorts of men, to hold their attention even when they weren't with you.

'You take it so very serenely,' said Ian oddly then, as he reached for one of her hands, cradling it briefly.

Their eyes met in perfect understanding. 'I've never been possessive of you.'

'I know,' he replied, gently squeezing her fingers. 'And sometimes I regret that very much.'

Then she smiled with affectionate malice. Given she didn't know whether it was directed at him, or herself. 'But only sometimes,' she said softly and returned the pressure of his hand quickly before withdrawing her hand. 'Only sometimes.'

He took her home, and they sat for several moments in his car, talking quietly. Then Ian told her, 'My attitude tonight doesn't mean a thing, you know. I hope that you'll continue to see me, Robbie. I enjoy being with you very much.'

She patted his cheek and opened her door. 'Ian,

you enjoy anything in a skirt,' she said, which made him laugh as he climbed out and saw her to her front door. He waited beside her, a dark, handsome, wholly likeable man, and she was very, very glad that she was not in love with him as she turned to face him. Being in love with Ian could break one's heart. 'Give me a call.'

He bent his head and pressed a gentle, firm kiss to the side of her mouth and then ran swiftly back to his car.

Tiredly, Robbie entered the house, locked the front door behind her, and made her way up the stairs. She creamed off her make-up with calm, deliberate finger strokes, brushed her teeth meticulously, and went to her room to slip into a cool, cotton nightshirt. Her window was shut, and the room felt stiflingly warm, so she went to thrust up the glass pane. A cool breeze wafted in and licked at her skin, making her sigh as she stared out at the blue and grey shadowed, familiar night.

Her fingers tangled in the sides of her nightshirt, and she looked down at her slim figure, suddenly, dully bitter. She raised her hands and cupped her slight breasts, touching at her nipples and then running her fingers down her slim waist and hips. No creamy, luscious body to adorn with extravagant nightwear here. No full, burgeoning breasts, or generous hips to incite a man to lusting passion. No enticing features, lustrous, beckoning eyes, or glossy falling curls for a man to bury his face into.

A hot wave of angry yearning trembled through her. She was a good friend, oh yes, she was a great, understanding pal to one and all.

Good sport, good listener, good for laughs. She
whirled and threw herself on to her bed, and drove
her clenched fist violently into her pillow while she
thought of the womanly ideal, satin creamy skin,
and the passion of men.

Her week went by much as the others had done
before it, though she couldn't seem to shake the
restlessness that had plagued her since Sunday
night. She worked hard, cleaned the house until it
was spotless, and trimmed and pruned outside
until Herb said he doubted anything would grow
again, and all this was in an effort to tire herself so
that she could sleep the night through.

Marilyn, her favourite co-worker at the restaurant, was having a birthday party that Saturday
afternoon and evening, and she had warned
Robbie well in advance so that she could sign off
work to attend. All the employees were invited,
and would show up either before or after their
shift if they had to work that day, and also
Marilyn's large family and circle of friends would
come. The blonde, a cheerful, unflagging extrovert,
turned thirty on Saturday and was determined that
the world should know it. She had confessed to
Robbie that she was expecting close to a hundred
guests when estimating the escorts and children of
the people invited.

Marilyn and her husband John had done quite
well for themselves, with a spacious house and
lawn, and a private swimming pool at the back.
Marilyn's waitressing job was more of a hobby to
keep her busy rather than any real need for the
money. Her main interests in life were her

husband, two children, and home, which she
loved to redecorate every year at great cost of
both time and money. Robbie had been advised
to bring her swimsuit and a change of clothes,
for the party would last from three in the
afternoon to well into the night, with food being
served the entire time.

Normally she would have enjoyed the prospect
of going to a party, but for some reason, she was
ultra-sensitive to the fact that she would be
attending alone.

But she was just good old Rob. She wished in an
explosion of fervency that she could show up with an
incredibly handsome, charismatic man in tow who
was obviously besotted with her and no one else. She
longed rather forlornly for a whirlwind romance.

She had breakfasted lightly and late, and
lounged dispiritedly in her chair at the table,
dawdling over a third cup of coffee. She moped,
her slim chin tucked into the heel of one propped
up hand, her lower lip thrust out in a dissatisfied
pout. Maybe she should really cut loose and
splurge on that vacation in the Bahamas about
which she secretly dreamed. Maybe she should buy
a new wardrobe. Maybe she should move.

A dark shadow fell over the table, and she
turned her head to stare broodingly at Jason as he
rapped on the glass door with the backs of his first
two fingers. 'It's unlocked!' she called out, loudly
enough for him to hear.

He came inside, thrust the door shut behind
him, and eyed her up and down as he commented,
'Sunny mood we're in today, I see. Got any more
coffee?'

'Help yourself.' She ducked her nose into her cup and finished hers. As he sat down beside her, he quickly searched her face with his vivid eyes, and though she was well aware of the perusal, she didn't care enough to change her countenance.

'I'm not sure I want to sit that close to you,' he told her, with a delicate shudder. 'The way you look, you might start frothing at the mouth and biting any moment now.'

After a moment, she asked, subdued, 'Do I look that bad?'

His brows shot up as he realised the depth of her dejection, and he said, quickly reassuring, 'No, of course not. I was just teasing. But I must say, you don't look very happy with your lot in life.' He raised his cup to his lips.

'Jason, I need a man,' said Robbie plaintively, and he spat coffee across the table. That made her laugh, and he wiped his mouth with the back of his hand while regarding her sourly, wheezing.

'That's right, laugh it up. You shouldn't say such things when I've just taken a drink,' he complained, as he rose to get a paper towel. After wiping up the spilt coffee, he sat down again while sending her an understandably wary look.

'I'm being serious,' she said, once again morose and watched him from under her brows as he gingerly gave his coffee a second try.

'Whatever do you need a man for?' he asked and then quickly added, with an irrepressible grin, 'I mean, aside from what obviously comes to mind.'

'I'm going to a party tonight, and I don't want

to go on my own,' she replied and heaved a great sigh.

'No problem. I can take you.'

'You?' she responded with astonishment. He was clad in his usual disreputable cut-off jean shorts, barefoot and bare-chested, sinuous muscles rippling under sleek tanned skin. His hair was quite short as if he had just recently had it cut, and it hugged his well-shaped skull attractively.

He winced exaggeratedly and then expostulated with some heat, 'Do you have to sound so unflatteringly amazed? I, too, have been known to date occasionally.'

'No, no, it's not that,' she replied quickly. 'It's just that I hadn't thought of you as a possibility. It's pretty short notice. I hadn't expected to find anyone to go with.'

The sardonic look that had appeared at her first, surprised exclamation disappeared, and he assured her, 'Well as it happens, I'm free tonight if you want me to accompany you.'

'Are you still seeing Linda?' The question slipped out before she knew it, and she could have bitten her tongue out.

Only a quick lift of his brows and a flicker in those light grey eyes acknowledged any response to her question. 'Off and on,' he said very casually. 'She's seeing quite a bit of Walsh lately.'

'She tells you about it?' Robbie asked, somewhat taken aback, and he gave her a secretive smile.

'Yes, she confides in me quite a bit,' he admitted while watching every nuance and change in her expression.

She swallowed and said hollowly, 'I see,' which

of course she didn't, and he made no effort to elaborate on the subject.

'I came over to tell you that I'm on holiday for two weeks now,' Jason told her, leaning back and stretching out his long legs. They collided with hers, and she hastily drew away from the contact, disturbed by the sensation of his warm, silken-haired calf against hers.

He was too observant, and to draw attention away from her sensitive reaction to his touch, she asked him, 'So what are you going to do with yourself?'

'I'm not sure yet. I thought that, if you'd like to, we could drive up to Sandusky and spend a day at Cedar Point.'

She brightened at the thought. 'That sounds fun.' It also brought back images of time past. When Jason had first obtained his driver's licence, they had spent months begging their respective parents to let them go up to the amusement park for the day. They'd had no apparent success until summer had arrived, and Herb along with Jason's parents had sat them down for a long, stern lecture about safe driving and good conduct. At the end of it, Mr Morrow had thrown Jason the keys of their second car, while Herb had given Robbie a few twenty-dollar bills for spending money. She and Jason had been wildly delirious with the unexpected freedom, and had spent the day on wild rides and laughter. When she had gone to bed late that evening, she had still been able to feel the motion of the roller coasters plunging up and down. It was a good memory.

'We'll plan on it, then,' he promised and rose to

take his empty cup to the sink. 'I'd better get busy.
I've used all the towels and wash cloths up at
home, so I guess I'll have to do some laundry,' he
told her with a grin. As she laughed, he asked,
'When does this party start?'

'Three o'clock. They have a pool, so bring your
swimming trunks and a change of clothes.' He
passed behind her, and as he went towards the
back door, she said softly, 'Thanks, Jason.'

He stopped, and she felt his lips press quickly
against the top of her head. It sent a glow down to
her toes. 'You're welcome, sweetheart.' As he left,
she sat for some time marvelling at the affectionate,
warm person he had become.

She reluctantly cleaned out the refrigerator, as it
was a chore she hated, and after giving the cubicle
a good scouring on the inside, she plugged it back
in and restocked it with the things she had stored
in their deep freezer. Then, checking her wrist
watch, she found that she had whiled away enough
time to start getting ready for the party, so she ran
upstairs quickly.

She wore her bikini under her cherry-red shorts
with a matching tank top, and she threw a thin
cotton skirt into a bulky shoulder-bag for later
that evening. She also tucked some lotion, a comb
and towel, and a few items of make-up into the
bag and then she put her brown hair back into a
short, sleek braid which would look neat for hours
and also keep the hair out of her eyes. After
thickening her lashes with waterproof mascara and
running a light coat of lip gloss over her well-
defined lips, she was ready and skipped downstairs
again.

Jason was talking to Herb in the living-room, and as she approached quietly from the open doorway, she took a few moments to observe him without being noticed herself. He stood straight and tall in a light blue, sleeveless shirt, with brief black shorts that ended high on his muscled thighs and hugged his slim hips tightly. His sleek, well-brushed hair shone brown and light gold, eyes bright and intelligent against the tawny background of his tan. Whereas she turned a deep, nutty brown in the summers, Jason turned golden.

With an odd thrill of shock, Robbie realised that while she had been bemoaning the absence of a sleek and handsome man in her life, Jason had been there all along, and he was suddenly, heartstoppingly, shatteringly, sexually attractive to her. It kicked into life in her chest, and she knew without a shadow of a doubt that she would never be able to act nonchalantly around him again.

He looked up and to her, a sudden, vivid gaze. Mouth straight and firm, unsmiling, he stared at her as she stood in shadow. She looked from his high, prominent cheekbones, down the lean curve of his cheek, to that strong jaw and the slim, muscled lines of his throat. Her mouth was dry, and she couldn't swallow.

Then her father looked up, saw her, and asked, 'Hiding in the hall for any particular reason?'

She shook herself and walked forward slowly. 'No, I just remembered that I haven't bought Marilyn a birthday present.'

'No problem,' Jason told her, running his gaze down her legs. Having gone half-dressed around him for most of her life, she suddenly felt as though she were practically naked and flushed uneasily. 'We can pick up something on the way. Are you ready?'

She met his gaze with her large brown eyes for just a moment and then had to look away, feeling exposed, feeling as though he must be able to sense what was throbbing in her so strongly. God, she would never be the same. 'Yes,' she replied quietly and turned back to head for her room.

'Where are you going?'

'I don't have my purse in this bag. We'll need some money for the gift.'

He walked to her in quick, long strides and curved his fingers around her forearm. 'Don't worry about it, I have money. Let's go.'

The weight and warmth of his hand was burning into her arm like a hot brand. He was near, so near, right beside her, and she could smell the faint, fresh scent of him. 'I'll pay you back later.'

He drew her to the front door. 'I said don't worry about it. Come on, I'm driving. Oh, for heaven's sake, Robbie, do you want to give me petrol money, too? Strain your imagination a little. Pretend this is a real, honest-to-goodness date if you can.'

That made her laugh, an uncontrollable, nervous burst of giggles as he thrust her outside none-too-gently, turned back to give Herb an exasperated glance, and then shut the door behind him.

Shopping for Marilyn's present was quickly and successfully concluded, and they were soon sitting in Jason's two-seater sports car, engrossed in the complications of wrapping the box in the confines of the car. Inside, well-packed, was a delicate crystal figurine that Robbie had fallen in love with as soon as she had seen it. Jason's head bent close to hers as he held patiently in place the overlying ribbon with a long forefinger while she tried to finish the last knot with some composure, agonisingly aware of every accidental contact with his skin, feeling stiff and awkward. She then fluffed up the canary-yellow bow.

'How does that look?' she muttered while holding the box out for contemplation.

'Lovely.'

Robbie looked at him and found his head still close, and his grey eyes looking at her instead of the package. He bent close and pressed his warm lips against her cheek and then pulled away before she had time to react. Then he briskly started the car and pulled out of the parking lot, while whistling tunelessly through his white teeth. She sat in a daze the entire way to Marilyn's house.

It was after three when they arrived, and cars lined both sides of the shady street by Marilyn's already full driveway. Jason had to park a little distance down the shaded street, and they walked back, Robbie carefully clutching Marilyn's present while Jason let his right hand ride attentively at the small of her back.

Music pulsed out of the open windows of the large, two-storey house they came to, and Jason had to knock several times quite loudly before anyone answered the door. Marilyn stood on the doorstep flushed and laughing and motioned them both in with a cheery greeting. Robbie handed her the wrapped present and introduced Jason, who smiled faintly at the older woman's frankly interested perusal.

'Honey, I haven't the time right now, but later on, I want you to tell me just where you found him, and if there are any more where he came from,' laughed Marilyn with a quick affectionate pat on Robbie's flushing cheek before whirling away. The blonde threw over her shoulder, 'Everybody's in the back garden or the pool, and John's out cooking hamburgers! There's food and drinks on the picnic tables outside ... help yourselves!'

Jason cocked a quizzical eyebrow at her. With an unconscious toss of her head and a sniff, she led him through the house, with which she was familiar, and to the back.

The noise hit them before they stepped outside. Noise spilling from the nearby, crowded kitchen, noise from the back garden, noise from the stereo speakers, and all of it was loud. It was a bit of a sensory overload to take in all at once, and Robbie paused with her hand on the back door's knob to tell Jason aggressively, 'You offered to come. I don't want to hear a single complaint, have you got that?'

Quickly he wore a suitably meek expression though his grey eyes were dancing. 'I'll have a good time, I promise!'

Her glance, thrown over her shoulder, was obviously doubtful, but she hauled the door open anyway and could only hope that he was right.

People were everywhere, sprawled on the grass, splashing in the pool, and gathered around the two picnic tables which were pulled together, end to

end, and filled to overflowing with all kinds of hot
and cold foods. Robbie was a friendly person by
nature, but quiet, and she found herself stepping
instinctively back at the sight, overwhelmed.

Then Jason's hand was at her back again, warm
and heavy and reassuring. He drew close so that
his hip brushed hers lightly, and as she looked up
uncertainly, he smiled down into her eyes. She
remembered then that if she didn't know everyone
at the party, Jason didn't know anyone. With
equilibrium restored, she reached around her back,
tucked her hand into his in a wholly natural way,
and took him over to meet John, Marilyn's
husband.

John Earhart was a big, laughing man with a
barrel-chest slimming to trim hips and thick,
corded thighs. He was blond like his wife, and
bearded, and when he saw Robbie, he abandoned
his hamburgers to approach and give her a bone-
cracking bear hug. She had to laugh, pleased, and
then introduced him to Jason while hoping
inwardly that they would like each other.

They did. John eyed Jason's slimmer figure up
and down once and held out his huge hand for a
quick, hard shake. The two men exchanged a few
comments while Robbie ran her gaze in awe over
all the people.

Suddenly she shrieked, grabbed John's other
hand while they both looked at her in bewilderment, and then flew to the two sizzling grills to flip
at the cooking meat frantically. The underside was
scorched to a dark brown, and John roared in
good-natured amusement. He walked over and
slapped her on the back.

'Now look at what you've done!' he told her, and blankly she did just that, staring in puzzlement at the grills. While she was wondering what she had done wrong, John whipped off his apron and tucked it around her slim waist. 'You've just got yourself elected for the job! I need to check to see how the beer is going, can you take over for me for a few minutes?'

She had to laugh and she agreed cheerfully enough, while Jason joined them and inspected the cooking meat with a somewhat predatory interest. John barrelled off with a quick white and yellow grin to them both, and for a few minutes Jason and Robbie stood talking quietly together, while she kept a close eye on the meat.

Then another waitress from the restaurant, a lively brunette named Casey with huge, overly made-up eyes and the morals of an alley cat, came sauntering up. She devoured Jason with an avid look and said, 'Hi, Robbie. Who's your friend?'

Robbie sent a quick, involuntary glance up to Jason's face, and found his grey eyes alive with a lazy interest as he perused Casey as thoroughly as she did him. Normally Robbie liked Casey well enough, but something pricked inside her with the sharpness of a needle, and she gritted her teeth, eyes glittering, as she briefly acquainted the two with each other.

Casey threaded her arm into Jason's with a coy, enticing smile, obvious aroused and on the prowl, and said brightly. 'It doesn't take the two of you to watch over the hamburgers. Robbie, while you're cooking, I'll just take Jason and introduce him around for you. You don't mind, do you?'

'Do I have a choice?' retorted Robbie, but because she said it so laughingly, so naturally and lightly, she wasn't taken at all seriously, and the brunette drew Jason away.

Left alone, she looked down at the half-cooked, half-raw meat sizzling hotly in the sun and scowled fiercely. She didn't see the quick, unreadable look that Jason threw over his broad shoulder before politely following the brunette towards a knot of people. All she could see in her mind's eye was the interested, sexual appraisal Jason had given Casey. All she could think was that this party wasn't fun, wasn't fun at all, and that she wanted nothing more than to go home.

CHAPTER FIVE

JOHN carried out two huge ice chests filled with beer to replenish the depleted supply, and she watched, fascinated by the big man's strength. He paused to talk to a few people while wiping his hand down the back of his blue shorts, and then he came back to divest her of her apron and spatula. He bestowed a hearty, cheek-tickling kiss upon her and then shoved her away, ordering, 'Go and swim!'

Robbie's footsteps, after the initial impetus from the push, lagged uncertainly as she looked around the large crowded yard for signs of Jason. She found him lounging indolently against a bordering fence with Casey in close attendance, slinking so near that her thigh brushed his while she said something in his downbent ear. They were with a small, laughing knot of people either leaning on the fence or sitting stretched out on the short cropped grass.

Something angry and energetic pulsed through her then. She would have done better had she come on her own. She turned away in a quick, impatient movement and eyed the swimming pool with a brilliant, hard look. It was full to bursting with all shapes and sizes of people, both large and small, but she was looking specifically at several muscular young men who were playing a riotous game of water volleyball.

She snapped out of her immobility and headed in quick, long graceful strides to the side of the pool where she kicked off her sandals after unbuckling the straps and then straightened. Fully aware of the interested glances being thrown her way, she looked up at the yellow sun and let the warmth cascade upon her face for a long moment. Then she reached with both crossed hands to her waist.

With a long, slow, sinuous movement, she raised her cherry-red tank top over her brown head. Silence fell over the masculine-filled end of the pool. She dropped the tank top to the grass by her sandals. Then she smiled and unzipped her shorts at the tailored waist to slide them down over her gently swelling hips in a smooth, provocative movement. They fell in a tangle at her slim ankles.

She might not be lusciously buxom, but she was sleek. Every line of her body was streamlined, graceful curves and long, long legs, tightly muscled and firm under supple, very dark skin. She drew back her slim arms and stretched lightly before walking to the edge of the pool.

She was very satisfied with the attention she had received from her audience, but as her back was to Jason, she wasn't to know that he had abandoned all pretence of listening to Casey, his golden-brown head turned towards her, his light grey eyes dilated and peculiarly intent on every single move she made. His expression was tight and blank.

Robbie waited until she had a large, open space ahead of her in the pool and then drew herself together for a powerfully executed swan dive. The cool wetness of the water suddenly surrounding her body was a shock from the sweaty warmth of the high summer sun, and she shot through the water very fast with the force of her entry. Then her impetus slowed, and she was carried buoyantly to the surface again where she shook the cascading wetness from her eyes and laughed at the nearby, watching man.

It was enough to draw him close, circling almost like a predatory shark while he laughed back and asked her name. A few more men drifted over, and soon she was ensconced in the volleyball game, swimming hard and playing enthusiastically. The men deferred to her with great enjoyment, for she was naturally athletic and gifted with good hand-eye co-ordination from her tomboyish days, and as aggressive as any of them. A few women in the yard nearby stiffened and gazed with sharpening eyes at their escorts and the game they had been too lazy to join, unwilling to mess up their looks while so many people were present.

The opposite team was serving, and Robbie played the net with two other men while four more were positioned strategically behind them. She squinted over to where she had last seen Jason and Casey, but they weren't leaning against the fence any longer. Then before she could look searchingly around, the black and white marked ball came sailing over the net. It flew high and slowly, and appeared to be coming just over her head.

The young man behind her, a dark, good-looking fellow who was a cheerful flirt, was suddenly close to her, his long body sliding against hers in the water, his hands fastening firmly at her slim waist. He shouted and heaved her high into the air, water falling all around in a brilliant, sunlit cascade while she laughingly but not very seriously tried to hit at the ball. To her amazement, her small doubled fist connected, and the ball shot over the net to splash into the space between two of their opponents who couldn't react fast enough. Robbie felt herself sliding back down, against his chest and unnecessarily close, but the attention was pleasant and good for her morale so she leaned against him for a moment while he slid his hands slowly to the front of her waist and held her close.

His head bent to her ear, and he seemed about to say something when a large splash of someone entering the pool engulfed them both. She spluttered and laughingly rubbed at her water-blinded eyes while her young admirer lost his slippery grip on her.

Jason surfaced just beside them then, golden skin sparkling wetly on broad, muscular shoulders. He shook his hair out of his eyes, threw a light, unsmiling glance behind her and slipped his hard arm around her waist to draw her away from the game. Nobody from the volleyball group disputed his actions.

But Robbie did. She was still resentful of his desertion earlier, and had only just begun to enjoy herself again when he had to interrupt. 'I haven't finished playing,' she snapped, with a glitter in her brown eyes that told him to beware.

He dragged her, floating on his arm like a piece of flotsam, to the edge of the pool where he let her go, only to place both hands on either side of her. He was standing, but she was out of her depth and had to hold on to one of his forearms since he wasn't giving her enough room to tread water. Her legs kept brushing against his, which were planted firm and still, and she was immensely disquieted to find that her breath was coming short and fast.

After searching her face with some shrewdness, Jason smiled at her, white teeth flashing, and he told her cheerfully, 'I just thought you might like some attention, since that was why you wanted me to come.'

'You offered to come, I didn't ask you!' she retorted and then shoved against his arm experimentally. It didn't budge an iota. 'Besides, since you went off with Casey, I've found that I can have a perfectly good time on my own, thank you very much.'

He cocked his head at her quizzically, his expression alive with amused interest, his grey eyes sparkling. She looked into that gaze and then pressed herself against the edge of the pool to avoid touching his wet skin. Something in his eyes was unsettling, intent. 'But you wouldn't want your male friends to think that the chase is free and easy, would you?' he asked, wickedly light. 'Let them know there's a little competition. I hear it whets the appetite.'

Her look to him was speaking as she replied drily, 'I don't see them exactly flocking to my side. You seem to have a distinctly off-putting air about you.'

Jason looked briefly, uninterestedly to his right where the volleyball game was still going on, but was now played with an air of absent-mindedness as several interested, speculative glances were thrown their way. 'I don't know,' he said consideringly. 'There are a few biting fish in the sea. What do you say? Shall we give them something to think about?'

'What do you mean?' She didn't know how to curb or hide her skittishness at his close proximity, and so she shoved once again, irritably, at his arm.

'I mean to indulge in a little pretence. Let's act as if we are really dating. Let's say I'm the jealous boyfriend.' Another gleaming smile as if it were all a big joke.

'But we both know that you're not,' she muttered and swallowed against the thought of it. Jason, aroused and angry, hauling her into his arms, driving his hungry mouth down. A bout of excited trembling shook through her.

'But what would I do if I was?' he asked softly, his question so close to her thoughts that she jumped violently. He brought one hand to the side of her neck. She held herself completely immobile, not even breathing for fear of giving her agitation away. Jason's eyes took on an electric quality, blazing vividly until she couldn't look away from his lean face. 'Mightn't I just possibly pull you close, like this, and kiss you long and hard in front of everyone? Mightn't I want to establish things beyond a shadow of a doubt to people like Casey, and your young, groping friend who's watching us so avidly now . . .'

He pulled close until she was gently sandwiched against the edge of the pool and his lithe, wet body. She stared up into his half-shadowed face, her eyes dazzled by the sun and the purposeful light in his eyes. He bent his head. She knew then

what he intended, and dropped her heavy lids over
her eyes and raised her lips to meet his.

The noise of the party faded from her awareness
until it was no more than a meaningless
background disturbance. Jason's lips caressed
hers, brushing, stroking, gently probing his way
into her warm mouth. The kiss deepened, and the
forearm she had been gripping shifted to her back.
As her handhold slipped, she automatically
clutched at his shoulders, his skin silken and
slippery under her wet fingers. He gathered her
against his chest until they were close together,
torso to torso, her legs between his. All she could
feel was the cool water lapping against her heated
skin and Jason everywhere, nothing to hang on to,
nothing to hold, nothing to touch but Jason.

His mouth slanted hard against hers, never
brutal, never overly amorous under the heat of so
many different gazes, but enticingly, lightly,
sensually teasing. He raised his head and her eyes
opened slowly to stare at him, blankly. Aware
shock rippled through her. She suddenly knew for
certain that he was as sexually attracted to her as
she was to him. It was in his tense body, the tight,
very controlled muscles, that look of banked-down
excitement in his vivid eyes.

She whispered thinly, without even being aware
of it, 'Oh, my.'

'That is what I would do, I think, if I were
jealous,' he said conversationally and then quickly,
uncontrollably, licked hs lips.

She looked away very fast at that and said
again, 'Oh, my. So many people are looking at us.
L-let go of me, please.'

'Don't run away from me, Rob,' he said quietly, one arm a tight band around her waist, the other coming up to stroke at her hair.

'You're scaring me.' Her face half-crinkled in distress, her stomach a queer, tight knot.

'No, I'm not. I haven't done a thing to you that someone else hasn't already. I've seen you before in your front porch, late at night, with your father sound asleep in his room.' She bent her head jerkily and pressed a hand against her mouth, flushing hot and dark. Who had he seen her with? Who had he watched kiss her, touch her hair? His low tone was intense, biting. 'No, I'm not scaring you, you're scaring yourself. What are you feeling, Rob? What's going through your mind right now? What's frightening you?'

Her head jerked to one side. 'Don't dig at me,' she hissed. 'Now for God's sake, let me go! I'm not going to discuss anything with you here, of all places!'

His intent expression eased slowly, and he shook himself as if he had just remembered where he was. 'Okay,' he said mildly, and his hold on her loosened so that she could wriggle away. He stepped back. 'We can always talk later.'

But she wasn't ready to think about that, as her face burned hot from both the sun's rays and her own inner reaction, and without replying she ducked underwater to swim away swiftly. Jason gave her time to get her composure back, and she swam a strenuous three or four laps so that she could avoid conversation with anyone else. When she was ready to climb out, he was there to give her a helping hand, his long fingers closing over

hers, his shoulder and arm muscles flexing as he
took her weight in one quick heave up.

They walked over to where she had left her
clothes, his a tidy pile close by, and while she drew
her tank top over her wet bikini and left her
shorts, until she was more or less dry, Jason did
the exact opposite, sliding his black shorts over his
brief, skin-tight swimming trunks while piling his
shirt and sandals with her things. She scrupulously
avoided getting too near him, which he noted with
a wry twist of his mouth.

'Are you hungry?' he asked, tilting his wet head
down to her in enquiry.

She took a deep breath and unconsciously held
it while she glanced over at the laden tables of
food. 'I'm starved,' she confessed, and so they
went to get something to eat.

After piling their paper plates high with
hamburgers and finger foods, they went back to
where they had left their clothes and shoes, and
settled on the grass. Jason made a second trip
for a can of beer for himself and a soft drink for
her. Then they munched in a strangely companionable silence, considering recent events, and
Robbie stole several quick, furtive glances at his
profile as he basked indolently in the sun. She
didn't think he was aware of her scrutiny, for he
gave no sign otherwise as he commented from
time to time on the various antics of several
children who dashed in and out of the different,
fluctuating knots of people and generally acted
as though they hadn't a lick of sense among the
lot of them.

Then he said, very quietly, without looking at

her, 'Am I so very different from who you thought
I was that you don't know me anymore?'

Her hand jerked as she reached for her canned
drink and the can fell over in the grass, the cola
bubbling out until she snatched it up again
quickly. She ducked her head, for he had turned to
stare at her, his eyes oddly darkened. His hair was
beginning to dry, the lock that fell on his forehead
a lighter golden-brown than the back of his head,
which was still wet and slicked down . 'Did I ever
know you?'

He held still and then after a moment said
heavily, 'I thought you did. Maybe I was wrong.'
Her eyes shot up sharply. His own head was
turned to one side, his expression tired and
discouraged.

Her heart went out to him and that odd, lonely
look of his. 'You've become so complex,' she
whispered and reached out to touch his bare knee.
His gaze shifted slowly and he stared at her hand
until she drew it back, self-consciously. 'I think
there's a lot more I could learn about you.'

A smile creased his features then, the slowest,
sweetest smile she had ever seen from him, and she
thought she could never look at his countenance
enough just then. Even after she rose to get herself
more crisps, which were her eternal weakness, and
after his smile had faded, a quiet, subtle look of
pleasure remained on Jason's face for a long time.

The late afternoon faded to early evening, and
John was seen to throw his apron way and leave
his job. Though Robbie and Jason were among the
younger of the couples present at the party, their
air of self-possession and quiet maturity had

several older employees from the restaurant
gravitating towards them, along with John and
Marilyn. The group discussed many topics while
watching their respective children with wearily
jaundiced eyes, some sitting in lawn chairs, others
sprawled in the grass like Robbie and Jason.

She noticed that Casey avoided the group and
would not meet her eyes, for which she was
thankful. Though she had known better, the other
girl hadn't, and had tried to attract Jason's
attention while under the impression that he was
romantically involved with her. She didn't care for
that kind of behaviour and she was unsure of her
ability to hide her distaste for the brunette in the
future. Sexual promiscuity was one thing, but
when hurting an innocent victim became a
possibility, it was no longer a question of morality,
but one of ethics.

After a time, Marilyn wiggled out from under
her husband's heavy arm and came to sit next to
Robbie in the grass. For someone who had just
turned thirty, the other woman looked remarkably
young, with blonde hair falling in her sea-green
eyes and a sprinkle of freckles across her pert,
small nose. She blew up with her lower lip stuck
out and sent a wayward lock of hair floating up. It
came right back down again into her eyes, and she
sighed in disgust while Robbie grinned.

'So, tell me all!' Marilyn said, settling back in
the grass as though intending to have a long chat.
'Where and when and how did you two meet?
Have you known each other long?'

Robbie was never so thankful that she tanned as
darkly as she did when she felt a wave of warmth

rising stealthily, insidiously up her neck. 'We're neighbours,' she replied nonchalantly.

'Well, that doesn't tell me much,' complained the blonde, who then shifted her gaze to Jason with pleasure. He was leaning back on his elbow, one leg stretched out flat, the other propped up, and he smiled lazily at the other woman while Robbie looked anywhere but at the two sitting so close to her.

'We've known each other for about twelve years, now,' Jason told Marilyn, who sighed dramatically while glancing back with dancing eyes to Robbie.

'So you two are childhood sweethearts? Oh, I think that's so darling!' A dark scowl began to form between Robbie's brows like a thundercloud, and it grew more ominous as Marilyn continued teasingly, 'Why, I can't think why you haven't told us all about Jason before this, honey! To think she's been keeping someone as luscious as you a secret all this time!'

With an understandably wary look to her, which she didn't catch, Jason replied carefully, 'It hasn't exactly worked out like that, Marilyn, so perhaps that's why Rob hasn't mentioned me before. I find that she is surprisingly reticent about all sorts of things.'

She threw him a dark, unfathomable look from under straight brows, which he returned blandly enough. But though Marilyn continued to stare at her interestedly and Jason fell suddenly, unbudgingly silent, she didn't say a thing, and soon the blonde left to check on her two children.

They stayed until after sunset, Robbie going to

Jason's car to retrieve her bulky bag so that she could change into her skirt while he slipped on his shirt, and at seven o'clock the two picnic tables were cleared only to be reset with new, different food dishes. There was a succulent fruit salad served in two boat-like sides of watermelon rinds, along with several trays of *hors d'oeuvres*, a huge platter of cold barbecued chicken legs, and several different kinds of cheeses set out with an assortment of fancy crackers.

Marilyn opened her gifts a little later on amidst a smaller cluster of people who emitted loud bouts of laughter at some of the humorous items she received. Her mother, a huge, sunny woman with a laugh that boomed out over everyone's except John's, had given her a frothy, provocative nightgown which would, when worn, leave little to the imagination. John was obviously delighted while Marilyn buried her reddening face into the material like a bashful bride at the uproarious approval that the gift brought.

Jason had his arm casually around Robbie's shoulders, and then he leaned close to whisper into her ear, his lips brushing the sensitive skin, 'Do they throw such extravagant parties each time there's a birthday in the family?'

She settled herself closer against him, fully aware of his body warmth through her thin clothing as she turned to whisper back quietly, 'I don't think so. Marilyn confessed to me that as she was having a rather hard time facing her thirtieth birthday, she decided to meet the fact with gusto rather than shrink from something she couldn't change. I think the party was a lovely idea.'

His hand tightened briefly on her shoulder as he replied softly, 'I do, too. Certain things in life are irrefutable, and it's best to face them squarely. Trying to avoid them simply dosn't work.'

She turned her head to look at him questioningly, but he was watching Marilyn open her last gift, and there was absolutely nothing to be read in his expression.

Soon after the gifts were opened, several people began to leave, though there would soon be a new wave of arrivals when the restaurant closed. The party, Robbie guessed, would go on until close to dawn. After a quick, low word to her, Jason rose to approach John, and the two men talked for a few minutes. She wandered over to the pool which was practically deserted, even though it was still warm from the sun's heat. She bent and dabbled her hand in the water idly, sending small rippling waves out and watching them reflect the outside lights, dark blue depth and sparkling white. Her short braid fell over one shoulder, still wet from swimming that afternoon, and she knew that when she let it out, she would have curls until she washed her hair.

Behind her, Jason approached with slowing footsteps until he was just behind her, watching her bent figure. She had her body folded into a surprisingly compact package, one slim, dark arm wrapped around her knees as she crouched, her sleek head bent. The position was not unlike many he had seen her in before, years ago, when tracing childish patterns in the dirt, with her nose peeling from sunburn and her skinny legs scratched and bruised. In his memory, she had always been

sporting some new scrape on her knees, but it
never slowed her up. Not once had she backed
down from a dare because she had been afraid.

And now time and maturity had fashioned those
same, long legs into sleek, curving, feminine grace,
with high delicate arches to her slim feet and trim,
shapely ankles. Her bone structure had always
been slight, prompting him to a protective urge
before he even knew he had one.

'Ready to go?' His voice came quietly behind
her, and she rose quickly and turned, holding out
her hand to shake it dry.

'Did you tell John good night for me?' she
asked, looking over at the hosting couple who
were, as usual, surrounded by people.

'Yes, and he doesn't want you to leave without
seeing him first,' said Jason with a slight smile. She
went over immediately to the blond giant who
wrapped his arms around her for a tight,
enthusiastic hug. John, like Marilyn, was a very
affectionate person.

'Come and see us again!' he boomed, shaking
Jason's hand vigorously. 'We enjoyed having you!
Take care of Robbie, here, she's just a little ol'
thing!'

For some reason, that made Jason laugh
merrily, and Robbie scowled at him half-heartedly
while they went through the house to the front. He
was probably remembering the times when she had
been as ready for a fist-fight as any boy. As they
walked down the quiet, dark street to his car, he
once again let his hand rest at the small of her
back. This, she reflected scathingly while feeling
surprisingly sensitive to the touch, from someone

who had once regarded females as anathema. She'd been okay despite the fact that she was a girl.

It was a balmy, clear night, and as they climbed into his sports car, they found the interior still hot, like the pool water, from the heat of the day. Down came the windows, and as Jason drove them home, Robbie let her hair out of the damp braid and ran her fingers through the wavy strands until it blew across her eyes, fluffy and refreshingly cool as it dried.

As they neared their neighbourhood, she asked quietly, 'Did you enjoy yourself today?'

He was unsmiling, seemingly remote until she spoke, his attention fixed on his driving and his private thoughts, but he flashed her a quick, albeit secretive smile as he replied, 'Yes, I did. I wouldn't have missed it for anything.' That made her blink. She certainly hadn't thought the party deserved that sort of praise. They stopped at some traffic-lights, and he turned his head to look long and lingeringly at her. His eyes reflected the street-lights, brilliant glassy white and red and green flickering shallowly over the normal grey. 'How about you, did you have a good time?'

'At first it was a bit much,' she admitted, turning away to stare out of her window. An incredibly noisy, battered car pulled up beside them, stinking of exhaust fumes, and a greasy, bearded man looked over at her, grinning. She glanced away quickly. 'There were so many people! I wonder how she got to know them all? But it was nice, and Marilyn was happy we came. She liked you.'

'That,' he stated with some dryness, 'was made abundantly clear. To be honest, though, I think she was prepared to like anyone you brought.'

After a moment, she said with a studied indifference, 'She wasn't the only one who liked you.' As his head shot around and he stared at her, wearing a queer expression, she could have kicked herself for saying such a thing. She didn't want him to think she was jealous. Nothing was further from the truth.

An impatient car-horn sounded behind them, and Jason's attention snapped back belatedly to the changed light and his driving. 'Casey was certainly a very attractive woman,' he said cheerfully. She clenched her hand and heard a very faint sound. With a terrible shock, she realised that she was grinding her teeth. 'But,' he continued, and this was with great emphasis, 'she came on strong enough to send me screaming in the other direction.'

Robbie relaxed and then had to laugh. 'You know what she does with another waitress, whom you haven't met yet?' she said suddenly. 'On the nights they work together, they watch the men who come into the restaurant and made bets on each one's occupation and yearly income. They also rate each for looks on a scale from one to ten. It's surprising how many they end up dating.'

'Good God!' he expostulated with horror. 'And you were callous enough to leave me alone with her?'

'As I recall, you were the one to leave, sweetheart, not I.'

'Well, it wasn't as if you minded.' He sent her a

look, which she didn't see. 'You sounded disgustingly keen for me to go.'

'Oh, sure, what else could I have said?' she retorted exasperatedly. 'I have to work with the girl—should I have been rude over something as stupidly unimportant?'

'Ouch!' He pulled into their side street and parked his car smoothly in his parents' driveway, turning to regard her with a smile. 'I believe I've just had my hand slapped sharply. Next time I'll know better.'

She opened her car door and climbed out while she tossed back, 'What makes you think there's going to be a next time?'

He climbed out also and slammed his door shut without replying to that last retort. She walked around the front end of his car and started towards her own house, which was dark. Her father would be in bed, as the time was nearing midnight, and he rose early to go to church. In fact, as she looked around, the entire cul-de-sac seemed secluded and dark, and Jason was walking towards her. Her hands began to shake.

'Whoa, hold up,' he said quietly, putting his arm firmly around her shoulders as he caught up with her.

'Thanks for taking me,' she said nervously, trying to pull away. 'I'm glad you enjoyed it, but you really don't have to see me to the front door.'

'Nonsense,' said he, with a shadowy, unreadable look. He kept a tight hold on her while determinedly walking with her across the lawn. 'Remember, we're pretending this is a real date.'

The last 'pretence' had nearly shattered her

composure. Her heart began to pound. 'Come on, Jason,' she said desperately. 'Don't be so silly. I'll see you later, good night.'

He stopped abruptly and drew her around, both hands heavy on her slim shoulders, compelling her to face him. 'All right,' he said very low and fast, and the words throbbed. 'Let's drop the pretence, shall we? Let's be truthful with each other. Let's tell each other what we feel, Rob. Are you ready for that?'

He made her feel so strange. He made her feel shaken by acting so oddly, so aggressively, so full of a tension she could dimly sense but couldn't understand. His hands on her body. The hot memory of his mouth on hers. The trembling he caused in her. She couldn't tell him what he was making her feel. She didn't understand it herself. 'I don't know what you're talking about,' she whispered.

'That's one of the few times you've ever lied to me.' His hand left her shoulder and slowly, deliberately tangled in her wildly blown hair. He drew her near with a gentle, inexorable insistence and started to bend his head down. She tried to turn her head away, but was caught, caught by his hands and his body, his lips slanting hard and rough over hers, caught by the shaking in her limbs and her own response.

She felt the faint rasp of his beard, the hard band of his arm crossing the back of her waist, his wet, warm mouth open and eagerly plunging, the shocking sensation of weakness at the back of her knees. Her hands curled into his shirt. His body heat seared her. His heart was racing against hers much too fast. His hand came around her waist, slid under her tank top, and cupped her breast.

Her head fell back. She made a sound, low and hoarse, at the back of her throat. His mouth left hers and slid down, open, tongue licking at her neck. It left a trail of first hot, then cold fire as the breeze brushed them both, and tangled her skirt in his legs. He slid his hard fingers under her swimsuit top and touched her nipple, his body taut.

It was too much. He pushed too fast; she was too shocked, not only by her own involuntary response, but also by his. She whimpered, feeling the beginning, strange ache in her loins and his own surging desire, and she tore out of his hold to put her back to him. There was a pulse-beat of silence. She ran shaking hands through her hair.

He moved jerkily, saying in a tone quite unlike him, 'Robbie . . .'

In a panic, frightened that he would touch her again, she broke into a run across her front lawn, stumbled through the unlocked front door, and slammed it shut behind her, pushing the bolt home. She raced up the stairs and fell into her room.

She was appalled, appalled; she didn't know what was happening to her, she didn't know how to take it. She couldn't recognise the Jason she knew in the shadowed, urgent man she had left on the lawn. She couldn't control her surging physical response to him and she shrank from the thought that he knew it. It was a base and powerful instinct, this sexual awakening of hers, and it frightened her to death.

CHAPTER SIX

SHE prepared for bed feverishly, crawled in between her cool sheets, and tossed and turned. No position felt right; she couldn't get comfortable. She was hot, too hot, and she threw off her covers in impatience. A quick whirl and she was standing to stride over to her window and throw it wide open. She placed both hands on the sill and took deep, steadying breaths. The wind licked against her brow, and the long, exposed line of her throat, feeling deliciously refreshing.

Her nightshirt fluttered against her slim legs. After standing for long moments with her eyes closed, she opened them to look around her, sighingly. In order to get the most advantage from the night breeze, she lifted a slim arm and tucked her curtains well back.

The moon shone clear and silvery bright, throwing a pearly luminescence over the shadowed lawn and street. She leaned her forehead against the wooden border of the raised window pane and wearily let her eyes wander over familiar trees, brushes, the driveway on which she had once played hopscotch. She was the stranger here, the one with unfamiliar thoughts and feelings. Everything else was the same as it had always been.

She looked at the nearby oak tree and let her eyes slide idly down its thick, mature trunk.

Suddenly her breath froze in her lungs, and her lips parted soundlessly. Not everything was the same. Not quite everything, for there was a shadow at the base of the tree, a quiet, unobtrusive, leaning shadow. It was in the form of a man, positioned so that he could stare up at her bedroom window, upon which the moonlight fell clear and unfettered. He must have seen her every movement, blurred though it would have been through the metallic mesh of her screen.

She trembled, licking at dry lips while heaving a deep, shuddering sigh. One hand rose slowly to touch at the cold screen in front of her. She could feel the tiny, bumpy pattern of the woven wires, such a flimsy separation between her and the free, outside air.

'Go away,' she whispered to the shadow, which was tugging at her silently. 'Go away.'

She rose late, tired after a restless night, and trailed downstairs in her thin bathrobe to see if her father had left any coffee on the stove. He hadn't and so she made a fresh pot and then trudged back upstairs to shower quickly and dress. The day was cooler than it had been for some time, and so she dragged on faded, tight jeans with a grey sweatshirt, which she rolled up at the elbows.

She had intended to do a little housework that afternoon before work, but she simply couldn't summon up the energy. With her second cup of coffee half-empty in front of her, she laid her head in her folded arms and closed her eyes. She was tired and lonely. She wanted comfort and companionship. She wanted to have a shoulder upon which she could lean her head, wanted to have someone in whom she could confide and trust. She had thought that she might have found such a person in Jason as they renewed their friendship, but every time she thought she had a good understanding of their relationship, it twisted into something disturbing and different.

She loved her father, but theirs was a relationship built on a mutual, affectionate distance. How in God's name could she confess to her parent the feelings that were stirring to life inside her? She simply couldn't.

She had other friends, of course. Marilyn, perhaps, was someone she could confide in, but she wouldn't. And the others were good for laughter and social outings, but there were certain things Robbie considered too private and simply didn't discuss. That was the heart of the matter. What she felt was too naked, too new. She could barely confront the unfamiliar sensations in herself without wincing, let alone have the courage to confess them to someone else.

Her slim shoulders slumped in a curve of dejection. Surely she was the odd one in this modern age of freedom and openness. Surely she was backward. Perhaps it was because her entire sexual education had come from health classes in school, and her own reading. Perhaps it was because she hadn't had a mother to influence her to femininity earlier. Whatever the reason, Jason must think her an utter fool for the way she was acting, and she supposed wearily that she was.

Jason stood outside the sliding glass doors, leaning on his upraised forearm as he stared in at

Robbie's slim figure. It was some time before he broke out of that watchful stillness to knock lightly at the glass.

Her head came up. At the sight of Jason just outside, dressed in much the same way that she was, her composure splintered and she turned away, her mouth shaking. Unseen to her, his head slowly bowed and a muscle twitched in the tight line of his jaw. That was the pose she saw when she gathered enough courage to face him.

Her eyes widened at his averted face, his downbent eyes, the tired curve to his firm, well-cut mouth. He looked as though he had slept as little as she. She rose and flipped the lock, watching the metal and glass slide open rather than look at his face as he stepped in. With a quick flex of his arm, he threw a mechanics handbook on to the dining table, and she flinched at the sharp slap it made as it landed. Then Jason slowly closed the door behind him.

'I thought I'd bring the book back I borrowed from Herb,' he said quietly, his head turned towards her.

She couldn't face him, she just couldn't. She walked to the open archway that led to the hall and put her hand on the wall. The conflicting impulses that were pulling her both towards and away from him were wearying her. 'He's gone to church,' she replied, and when he didn't respond, she said almost absently, 'But you knew that.'

'Yes.' She thought his voice sounded thin, stretched tight, tired. Then he gentled audibly as he asked, 'You can't look at me, can you? What's wrong sweetheart?'

Tears blurred her vision unexpectedly and she blinked rapidly. Her sleek head bowed, and she didn't have the will to keep the words from tumbling out, 'I'm lonely.' The last syllable quavered, and she heard him move behind her, a quiet cloth rustle that made her visibly jump. He instantly, totally stilled. She whispered, 'I thought . . . I thought I didn't know you, but I find I don't even know myself any more.'

Jason said sighingly, full of emotion, 'Oh, Robbie.'

'I don't know how to handle, uh . . .' she tried to say, the words trembling with the difficulty. '. . . I don't know how to . . . talk about what I'm feeling. I don't know how to stop us losing what friendship we have . . .'

He shifted again, and she turned to see him leaning against the dining table, his hands splayed out on the surface, shoulders hunched, head averted. As she watched, he moistened his lips and whispered, 'My feelings for you aren't going to change if that's what you're afraid of.' He lifted his head and met her brilliant gaze, and he smiled but it didn't reach his weary eyes. 'I'll love you no matter what you do, Robbie, and I'll be whatever kind of friend you want me to be.'

A tear spilled over and ran down her cheek. He closed his eyes tightly against the sight, and as she raised her hand to wipe at the wet streak, she confessed with a wobbly little laugh, 'My nose is running.'

He glanced around the room, found a nearby box of Kleenex sitting on the kitchen counter, and brought it to her silently. While she bent her head self-consciously and blew her nose, he set the box aside and then turned back to her. He asked diffidently, strained, 'May I hold you?'

She was unprepared for the way his quiet, somehow lonely question would make her face crumble. He had her in his arms in a quick, long stride, and her head sank to his shoulder. Such warmth, he had an enormous capacity for gentleness which amazed and humbled her every time he showed it to her. Just when she thought he was strained to the limit, he reached deep inside himself and gave her more.

With one hand he cupped the back of her head and rocked her very slightly. He brought his head down and laid it on her shoulder while her arms slid sneakily around his trim, tight waist. For the first time, she began to wonder if he was as shaken by his own physical desire as she was by hers. She was astonished to find the comfort she thought she never would, and she slipped one arm around his neck to hold him tight.

After a long, wordless moment, he raised his head again and blindly searched for her lips. She tilted her face up and met his seeking mouth, letting hers fall softly open. He fervently, lusciously, moistly kissed her until she was gripping the back of his head with both her hands, losing all sense of balance. His arms were wrapped around her, two taut hard bands, and he moulded her sagging, trembling figure to him, a hand at the small of her back pressing her hips to his.

She was hot and aching, and she dragged her mouth away from his to moan, 'No.' He didn't appear to hear as he buried his mouth against the

racing pulse-beat in her neck. Her hands, which
had held him so insistently just a moment before,
twisted into the shirt material at his shoulders. She
said raggedly, 'Jason, Dad is going to be home any
minute now.'

A quick tremble shook through his frame, but in
the next instant he was letting her go and stepping
back almost calmly. She had to stare at him,
astounded, for nothing showed in his expression
except calm, normal cheerfulness. But when she
looked into his grey eyes, they glittered.

He turned away, a quick whip of his body. 'I see
you've got coffee made,' he said easily. 'May I help
myself to a cup?'

'Of course.' Her lips felt swollen, unwieldy, and
she licked them self-consciously. 'I'm going to
the bathroom. Would you warm up my cup for
me?'

'Sure.'

In the small, downstairs cloakroom she ran cold
water into the sink and splashed at her face. There
was a dark flush along her cheekbones, and a
bruised look to her lips. She held cold fingers to
her dry eyes for a long moment and then reached
into the cabinet behind the mirror for a few
aspirin, which she shook out and swallowed
without water. Then she took the comb she stored
in the cabinet and straightened her hair, before
walking back to the kitchen.

Thus it was that when Herb walked into the
house, some ten minutes later, he found Robbie
and Jason lounging at the kitchen table with all
appearance of normality. They both looked tired,
though, and Jason's short cropped brown hair was

mussed as though he had dragged his hands through it repeatedly.

Herb said with joviality, 'Looks like you two had some time at that party last night.' He went over to the coffee pot to pour himself a cup, totally missing the odd, skittish glance the other two shared behind his back.

'I suppose you could say that,' responded Jason, with some dryness.

She yawned and slumped in her chair while rubbing her eyes. 'At least you don't have anything to do for the rest of the day,' she muttered and sipped at her coffee. 'I have to work tonight.'

'Poor baby,' mourned Jason, eyes dancing vividly. She stared at him with pleasure at the return of his usual good spirits and felt her own lifting in response

Herb returned to the table and sat down, both men obviously waiting for her reply to Jason's teasing. She buried her nose in her cup and murmured composedly, 'You always were an unsympathetic brat.'

Work was surprisingly easy to get through, despite how tired she felt. She waited on pleasant, interesting people which made serving them easy, and in return received handsome tips for her own good humour and consideration. Casey also worked that evening and Robbie found herself behaving quite naturally towards the other girl, who was understandably wary at first. In light of her recent encounters with Jason, the brunette's behaviour seemed unimportant, and gradually

Casey's manner warmed to her until the other girl
apologised.

'Forget it,' was Robbie's cheerful advice. 'There
was no harm done.'

Casey's piquant face flushed darkly, and she
could not meet Robbie's eyes. In a rare burst of
honesty, she replied, 'But that isn't any credit to
me, is it? I shouldn't have done it, Rob. You
deserve better treatment than that.'

The other girl walked away quickly, while
Robbie stared after her bemusedly. They never
spoke of the incident again, and Casey continued
to behave much as she ever had. But she never said
anything catty either to Robbie's face or behind
her back, and Robbie in turn treated the brunette
with special kindness.

Business picked up towards the end of the
evening, which was a bit odd for a Sunday, and it
was quite late before Robbie was able to drive home
in a tired daze. As she pulled into the driveway and
then the garage, she thought that she would be able
to sleep well if her present exhaustion was any
indication. She completed her nightly routine in a
leisurely fashion, dressed for bed, and wandered
around her bedroom, putting away the clothes she
had worn that day. Soon she was flipping off her
light and turning down her covers when the dark
purple images of last night disturbed her thoughts,
and she turned to the window to obey an impulse she
only half understood.

Standing at her window, which was closed now
against the unseasonable coolness of the night, she
let her eyes wander dreamily down the oak tree she
had climbed a thousand times in the past. He had

stood under the tree after kissing her good night, after touching her breast.

Her heart gave a great, painful leap, and she trembled so that she thought her legs might collapse. The shadow, the waiting, watching, wakeful shadow in the night that had so haunted her dreams was back. She would have sworn he wasn't there when she drove up, so he must have looked for her return. She could almost see what his grey eyes would look like, even from that distance. They would glitter like dim silver. They would be filled with the same bright desire she had seen in them just that very morning. They would be silently compelling her to make the choice he would never outwardly press her to make. She was well aware that he knew she saw him. He would have sensed it from her long, wordless stare down at him the night before, from her obvious exhaustion that morning. He would be able to see her even now, for the moon was still bright and strong, and the curtain trembled violently from the force of her spasmodically clenched fist.

Oh God.

The next few days followed much the same pattern as Sunday. Robbie drove herself into a frantic whirlwind of activity, shopping, afternoon matinées, house-cleaning, work. The few times she had seen Jason were brief and filled with a friendliness that overlaid watchful wariness on both sides. His subtle relentlessness sent her into a wild panic. Every night the shadow watched her window from under the oak tree's swaying branches, and she couldn't sleep.

And when she did, she dreamed of a dark pursuit. Vague, restless images pervaded her sleep and made her toss and turn. She was always hot, sweating, and she lost her appetite. Each unexpected noise made her jump violently. Each of her senses was heightened to an unbearable pitch.

Wednesday she was simply too listless to do anything before going in to work that evening, and so she dragged out the lounge chair and spread her bikini-clad figure liberally with lotion. Then she stretched out to bask in the sun's fierce rays while attempting to read the latest paperback she had bought. She found her eyes wandering over the lawn instead of the open pages in front of her, and she jerkily lifted one slim hand to her mouth, gnawing at a fingernail.

Jason came out of his back door and casually strolled her way, his hands tucked into the back pockets of his faded jeans. He had no shirt or shoes on, and she was intensely aware of every fluid, muscular movement as he jumped over the dividing fence and approached.

'Hello,' he said cheerfully, throwing himself on to the grass beside her and tilting his head to squint at her sideways. He wore a slight, wry smile on his lips which widened as she found herself tangled into staring helplessly at the thin sheen of sweat that beaded on his strong, graceful collarbone and chest.

She jerked her gaze away and blindly looked at her book. 'Hello, yourself.'

His long arm reached over to her and plucked the book from her hands, asking, 'What are you reading?' His hard fingers brushed against hers and she jumped. Then, with his head bent as he scanned the cover and inside flap with seeming interest, he said quietly, 'You look tired, Rob. Haven't you been sleeping well lately?'

Her brown eyes smouldered with frustration. He, too, looked a bit worn, with the tiny lines at the corners of his eyes and mouth deepened slightly, but he was much calmer than she. 'I've been sleeping perfectly well,' she snapped and chewed at her thumbnail.

He glanced over at her, quick and bright, before placing the book gently on the ground and reaching over to draw her hand away from her mouth. 'And you're nervous, too, I see,' he said softly. Their eyes met. His shone like silver as they ran over her taut, slick features intently. His big body was half-twisted towards her as he knelt up on one knee. Those lovely, naked shoulders were just within reach to stroke if she wished. Her hand, still captured in his, shook. He whispered lightly, 'So very, very nervous. What's on your mind, sweetheart?'

'Go to hell,' she said through stiffened lips, and she tried to drag her hand away. His fingers tightened insistently on hers.

'Not very friendly today, are we?' He brought her hand up and bent his head to place a kiss at the inside of her wrist. At first she couldn't move, but the sudden sensation of his tongue licking at her salty, sweaty skin had her thrusting the fingers of her free hand into the hair at the back of his head. She tugged none too gently, pulling him back up.

'You're playing a game with me,' she gritted,

angrily leaning forward to stare at him, eye to eye.
'For some reason you've decided that you want me
and so you're using every opportunity to push me
into giving in to you.'

'Why, sweetheart,' said Jason blithely, 'what am
I doing to pressure you? I've barely touched you,
and I certainly haven't talked about any such
thing, have I? What is it that I've done that
bothers you so terribly?'

Her eyes went wide. He hadn't really done anything that would have affected her had she been
indifferent to him in the first place. He was
working upon her own emotions and desires, and
there was nothing of which she could rightly
accuse him without exposing herself. She gave
herself away at every turn.

She pushed away from him, and he let her go.
Whirling to her feet and taking a few impatient
strides away, she snarled angrily, 'I have no
intention of doing a single thing I don't want to,
do you hear?'

'You have made it abundantly clear,' he replied
drily, squatting back on his heels as he watched
her agitation.

She spun on her heel to face him again. 'Then
let up on me!' she cried explosively.

His face, his eyes, his stance, his voice were all
implacable as he shook his head and whispered,
'No.'

She whitened as if struck. 'You're going to lose
my friendship. You're going to drive me too far.'

At that he smiled gently and repeated, 'No. The
conflict is all within yourself. You can't place the
blame on me for what you're feeling.'

She bent her head and rubbed her eyes wearily with thumb and forefinger. She felt exhaustion seeping into her limbs and mind, clouding her perspective, confusing her. 'Damn you, why?'

'You said it, yourself, Robbie,' he replied and straightened. Something throbbing crept into his voice. 'I want you.' She covered her face with her hands at his bald statement. 'Are you busy tomorrow?' he asked suddenly.

Her head lifted fractionally. 'What do you have in mind?' she returned with some wariness.

His bare shoulders and chest shook in a silent chuckle. 'I thought we could go to Cedar Point, if you'd like to. I hear that the weather is supposed to be sunny.'

She lifted her heavy gaze to his face and stared at him blankly. Here she was, tormented by the newly born desire she felt for someone she had always considered as a brother. Here, she was, a skittish virgin, struggling to comprehend her feelings of friendship and feelings of sexuality towards this young man, who had no difficulty at all meshing the two together in his mind, and flitted without apparent effort from one aspect of their relationship to the other. What was the secret? How did he do it? Was the act of mating as casual as that in his mind? Was it so important, in hers?

Yes.

After standing patiently as the moments ticked by, searching her face and trying to read the strange expressions that raced across it, Jason commented, his tone mild, 'I wasn't aware that it was such a difficult decision.'

'What? Oh, tomorrow,' she replied, pretending to be absent-minded when in actuality she was aware of every move, every breath, every expression of his. 'Sure, I'll go. I didn't have anything else planned.'

'Such enthusiasm,' he muttered sardonically.

They made plans then, casually snapping at each other as though they were indeed brother and sister, and Jason took his leave. By that time, the afternoon had advanced so that she had to get ready for work. She carted the lounge chair back inside, showered and changed, and then left a note for her father before leaving the house. In it, she explained her plans for the next day, for she doubted if she would see him before tomorrow night, if then.

She took the drive to the restaurant in a daze, unaware of the green atmosphere around her or of the mellow brilliance of the late afternoon sun which promised a glorious sunset as it sank towards the west.

Her mind definitely wasn't on her work, either, as she punched her time card in and donned her frilly apron. Her mind was filled with faceless, formless shadows, with Jason and his inexplicable attitudes and mood changes, with her own confused longings and ideals.

There wasn't any question in her mind that she wanted Jason. But part of the problem was that she fully expected to meet a man with whom she would fall in love. She wanted to marry. She liked the idea of having a life-partner. Though she wasn't necessarily looking for marriage, it was lurking at the back of her mind whenever she was attracted to someone. How could she allow herself to get tangled into this physical attraction for Jason?

It wasn't as if there was anything wrong with him, she conceded silently, as she flew back and forth and mixed up her order, generally making a mess of her station. He was good-looking. He would make someone a wonderful husband some day. He was strong, reliable, and had everything going for him. His future was tremendously exciting to contemplate. But he was Jason, the boy next door, the dirty, skinny ruffian who used to plague her to no end. He was the one who had thrown leaves in her hair, who had stuffed moss in her tennis shoes, who had treated her with insufferable condescension.

But when he was with her, all such thoughts flew out of the window. He stood upright and tall, with that lovely, lean, muscular body which fascinated her so. He made retorts with biting sarcasm, he listened to her with the patient wisdom of one far older, he gave her a devastating, rare honesty, was remarkably supportive. And when he kissed her, she lost all self-control.

She was being stupid. No one saved themselves for marriage anymore, not in this day and age. They took love where they could find it. They were pragmatic and said goodbye when the time came. They understood conflicting loyalties and ambitions and realised that sometimes love wasn't forever.

There was nothing wrong with taking what she wanted from Jason, except for the fact that she was afraid she might not be able to leave it at that.

She was afraid that she might want something more, might become so entangled with infatuation for him that she would lose sight of what she wanted.

Heaven help her when she really fell in love.

The restaurant was frantically busy. When Robbie finally took her supper break, she was too tired to even think about eating. She put her head down on the table and dozed until Marilyn shook her shoulder, informing her that it was time to get back to work.

'Are you all right?' asked the blonde with some concern, for Robbie was pale and unusually lethargic.

'Oh, I'm fine,' she replied with a yawn as she forced herself to stand. Her head ached dully, and her legs felt like used rubber. 'I haven't been sleeping well the last few nights, and it's beginning to catch up with me, that's all.'

'Hmm. Well, you don't look okay. You look awful,' was Marilyn's rather tart reply. 'Maybe you'd better have another cup of coffee before getting back to work.'

She had to laugh. 'If the three cups I've already had don't help me, then nothing will! Have any of my tables left?'

'Yes, and your tips are in a coffee-cup, by your station. You've just got a new table. I've set them up with water. They should be ready to order in a few minutes.'

She groaned and rubbed her eyes. 'Well, thanks. I knew it would be too much to hope for things to slow down this early!'

'Nothing's wrong, is it?' asked Marilyn, looking

down as she made a great fuss about straightening her apron. 'Are you still seeing Jason?'

The other woman's question startled Robbie unduly, and she replied with too much emphasis, 'Jason and I were never really dating. He kindly escorted me to your party, but really, there's nothing between us!'

'Oh!' Marilyn was flustered and made some effort at recovery. 'Oh, I see. I hadn't realised. Things looked a bit . . . well, different at the party.'

For some reason, that brought to mind the time Jason had kissed her in the pool, and her face flushed scarlet. 'Well, we're close friends, so it might be easy to think we're romantically involved,' was all she could think of to say.

'I see,' repeated Marilyn slowly, eyes shrewd as she took in Robbie's heightened colour.

But Robbie knew very well that the older woman didn't see at all and instead of trying to explain the intricacies of a relationship she didn't understand herself, she gave it up and went back to work.

What followed soon afterwards was predictable, in the light of her own preoccupied exhaustion and the frantic pace of that night. What followed should have been expected, as a hurrying waiter spilled water on one of the few steps that led down to the secluded section of the restaurant that was Robbie's station. He rushed to the back for a cloth, anxious to mop up the water before someone slipped and fell.

Which was just as Robbie was coming out to take up her station again, tired, with slowed reactions, anxious to get the evening over with so that she could go home. As she went down the steps, her foot slipped on the spilled water, but she moved too slowly to catch herself. She saw herself fall almost in slow motion down the rest of the stairs.

Her foot turned underneath her, taking her entire weight, and she crumpled to the floor. She didn't even scream. She was too busy grabbing for the ankle on which she had so agonisingly landed, her face a paper-white mask.

CHAPTER SEVEN

EVERYTHING that followed her accident was a new experience for Robbie, who had never suffered anything more than a pulled muscle in her entire life. For a moment, nobody even noticed her sitting so quietly on the restaurant floor, doubled over her awkwardly-bent leg.

Then she heard someone utter a shocked exclamation, and chairs scraped across the floor as a young couple seated at a nearby table saw her and came over concernedly. 'Are you all right, honey?' asked the brunette anxiously, as her husband knelt on the floor.

'I'm not sure,' she said quite calmly and began to shake. Sharp needles were piercing up the length of her leg. The man held his hand out solicitously and helped her to stand on her good foot. Determined to make light of her fall, Robbie tentatively tried to put her injured one to the floor, and the gentle contact caused such excruciating pain that she nearly fainted. The woman went to find the manager, while her husband carried Robbie to a nearby chair. Soon her plight was being discussed over her bent head, while she heard and saw everything around her as though it were filtered through a crimson haze. When the young woman had returned, she insisted on Robbie drinking her glass of wine. The logic of that escaped her admittedly limited thinking at that moment, but the wine was cold and refreshing so she didn't argue.

Marilyn came over quickly, attracted by the ruckus, and she immediately offered to drive Robbie to the emergency ward at the nearest hospital, which the manager was quick to accept. It solved his dilemma nicely, for he had conflicting responsibilities both to see to the welfare of his employees and also to keep the restaurant running smoothly.

He carried her out to Marilyn's car, and though the trip to the hospital was short, it seemed like an eternity to her as she battled through every moment of pain. Her ankle had swelled rapidly to alarming proportions, and she could only hope that she hadn't broken it.

At the hospital her ordeal grew much easier as she was given something for the pain. The crimson-like haze faded to a bearable, muddled fog, Marilyn called her father while she was taken for X-rays to determine the damage done by her fall.

The young doctor in attendance treated her with a calm, matter-of-fact manner which was remarkably steadying. After he had carefully studied the X-rays of her slim ankle, he became brisk and cheerful. 'You're a very lucky young woman, you know that?' he told her as she sat, white under her deep tan. Her eyes were enormous, dilated from the shock and the medication, and they sparkled liquid-bright as she stared at him. She was slow to react.

'Oh?' Her voice was a thin, calm thread of sound. 'Pardon me if I don't feel so lucky at the moment.'

He came close and with cool, hard fingers clasped her ankle and foot in his hands. Even that gentle touch throbbed up her leg like fire, despite the medication. She paled even more and fixed her gaze fiercely on a point just behind the doctor's white-coated shoulder.

'Well, you should be glad to know that you didn't break any bones. You simply have a very bad sprain. I'm going to wrap it now, and the bandage is going to feel tight because your ankle has swollen so much. Keep it wrapped for a few days, preferably a week if you can manage it, and stay off your feet as much as possible.'

'So much for work,' she muttered and rubbed at her aching temples with her fingers.

'Oh, yes. You're the waitress, right? I suggest you refrain from working for a few weeks. If you go back to work too soon, you'll be doing yourself more harm than good.'

He proceeded to bind her ankle tightly, which made her bite her bottom lip so hard that it bled. Afterwards, he wrote her a prescription for pain medication, and she was efficiently settled into a wheelchair and pushed out to the hall, where she found her father sitting with Marilyn, his hair rumpled and his clothes hastily donned. Under his summer jacket, she caught sight of his nightshirt.

The look of concern on Herb's face had her eyes filling with weak, absurdly easy tears, but she determinedly blinked them back while the doctor cheerfully assured the other two that there wasn't a thing to worry about. As Marilyn had provided the ward clerk with the necessary insurance information which the restaurant manager had given her, Robbie was free to leave with her father. Marilyn stayed long enough to make sure she was settled as comfortably as possible in the back seat of her father's car, leg stretched stiffly out and the injured ankle propped on the seat. Then she left, with the assurance that she would call at the house the next day with Robbie's bag, which had been forgotten in the earlier confusion.

By the time Herb pulled into their driveway, it was very late and Robbie's brown head had slumped to one side in exhaustion. The medication had taken the edge off her pain, but she was still extremely sensitive to every bump in the road and she was weary from bracing herself against the jolts.

Her father carried her into the house and up the stairs, joking that he hadn't done such a thing in a good fifteen years, which made her grin lopsidedly. The last time he had carried her, she'd been a good sixty pounds lighter. He deposited her carefully on to her bed and stayed long enough to see that she had her nightshirt and was capable of changing for bed by herself, and then he left again to fill her prescription at the local, all-night drug store.

She was determined to stay awake until he returned but after gingerly settling herself in bed, her eyelids promptly fell shut, and she was soon deeply asleep, despite the constant nagging ache in her ankle and the fact that her bedroom light was still on. She didn't stir when her father checked her room briefly after he returned, tucking the covers up to her shoulders as tenderly as any mother before leaving again and turning off her light.

Two things woke her up late the next morning after a deep, yet troubled sleep. One was the pain in her ankle, which was so stiff and swollen she was wholly unable to bend it at the joint, and the other was a hot, dry, cottony feeling in her mouth. She desperately needed a drink.

For a few moments, though, she simply stared around her bedroom. The sun was high and bright, an indication of the late hour, and the light spilled through the curtains at her window in a golden beam. She wondered if her father had taken time off work to stay with her, like he used to when she was too ill to go to school. She felt guilty for being such a bother and at the same time hopeful that he hadn't abandoned her for the day. She was sure he wouldn't.

'Dad?' she called, her voice blurry with sleep. At first there was nothing but deep silence, so she called again, louder this time, with some uncertainty.

She felt absurdly comforted when she heard footsteps sounding heavily on the stairs, and she struggled to a sitting position, wincing as she jarred her injured foot.

When Jason walked through her open bedroom door, she was pushing her tousled brown hair off her forehead, one side of her face creased with delicate lines from her heavy sleep, her eyes blinking and bemused. Her nightshirt was twisted at her torso, and the bedcovers were rumpled around her slim hips. When she looked up and saw him, surprise and dismay flooded her features at the same moment.

'Oh, no!'

He was casually dressed in worn Levi's, with a plain white shirt rolled up at the elbows and blue tennis shoes. He looked fresh, alert and incredibly vibrant, and he grinned at her exclamation, swift and bright, as he walked into her room. 'What an awful greeting, you ungrateful creature!' he teased, sitting on the edge of her bed as his eyes smiled at her. 'If you want me to go away, just say so, though I might warn you, I'm the only help you've got at the moment. Your father's gone to work.'

'I've just remembered,' she muttered morosely, as she sank back down on her pillow and buried her chin into her chest. 'We were supposed to go to Cedar Point today.'

Her depression was so obvious, he reached out a large hand and tucked her hair gently behind her ear. 'We can go another day,' he assured her, letting his gaze roam freely over her half-covered figure. There were dark circles underneath her eyes and a tautly etched expression that hinted at her acute discomfort. Her full, lush mouth was turned down in a disconsolate bow.

She fought a brief, intense struggle and then gave in to petulance. 'But I wanted to go today.'

He laughed quietly and shifted his weight so that her bedsprings creaked. 'And here I was thinking that you had thrown yourself down those stairs just so that you wouldn't have to go with me,' he teased. She couldn't meet his brilliant gaze and was appalled when her chin started to quiver uncontrollably. He sobered instantly and put his hand heavily on her shoulder. 'I was only joking, Robbie.'

'Don't you think I know that?' she whispered,

frustrated with herself, and she turned her eyes away to sigh. She bent her head in a weary gesture and rubbed the back of her neck with her hand.

His question was gentle. 'Are you in much pain?' After a moment, she gave a reluctantly honest nod, and his hand squeezed tightly on hers before he stood. 'Then I'll go get your pain medication and a glass of water, all right? And after that's had a chance to take effect, we'll see about getting you dressed and downstairs.'

He was quick and he stood frowning down at her as she popped two pills into her dry mouth and then greedily gulped down the entire glass of water. Then he helped her to the bathroom, waited outside until she had finished, then carried her back to her bed. While she watched and directed, he moved around her room to draw out bright shorts and a comfortable top. He opened her lingerie drawer and rummaged for a pair of panties, his head bent, his broad, well-shaped back to her. She was not so preoccupied with her painful ankle that she wasn't embarrassed by that, a slow, dark flush rising over her neck and face at the sight of his large masculine hand holding a handful of fluffy white nothings.

When he turned around with a complete outfit in his hands, she was looking down fixedly at the print border of her top sheet, furious at her own lack of mobility and extremely self-conscious with Jason in her room. At first she hadn't been, for he had seen her looking far worse than she did at the moment. She had felt perfectly normal and acted quite naturally, until she noticed his vital, mature maleness, as though for the first time.

He walked over and tossed the things down to her. They fell in a flutter all over her covers, and as she refused to look up, he said quietly, 'I'll be just outside the door if you need any help. Let me know when you're ready.'

As soon as the door had closed behind him, she pulled the shorts awkwardly over her ankles, cursing at her own clumsiness when she yanked her injured foot painfully. Then she balanced like a stork on one leg to get them drawn over her slim hips. The sleeveless shirt was the easy part, and with her hair even more wildly tousled, she called out, 'I'm done!'

The doorknob turned and he entered again, took one look at her, and went to her dresser top for her hairbrush. He sat on the edge of her bed again, ordered her to turn around, and set about getting the tangles out of her brown hair. That flustered her even more than his rummaging through her clothes had, and she snapped with a great show of irritability, 'My hands weren't injured, you know!'

'Oh, shut up,' he said and continued to brush her hair.

He was quite gentle, and the long soothing strokes through the soft brown length felt good. She muttered under her breath without much heat, 'Stubborn.'

'And you're a spoiled brat.'

She hadn't thought he'd heard her, and she roused at his response. 'I am no such thing!'

His hand clamped down hard on her upper arm. 'Sit still. You are. You always have been, and I've spoiled you as much as anyone else has.'

'Hah,' she retorted bitterly. 'I supposed you think you were doing me a big favour when you pulled all those pranks on me.'

He grinned unseen by her. 'You know you loved every bit of it.'

'For heaven's sake!'

He conceded, 'Well, at least you loved the attention.'

'I most certainly did not!' was her indignant exclamation to that.

'Of course you did. Now, that was your own fault. If you had sat still like I told you, it wouldn't have hurt.' She put a hand to her stinging scalp and tried to think of a suitable retort.

'I suppose you'll be saying next that I enjoyed having that frog you put down my back,' she muttered, her voice losing its bite as he set aside the brush and started to stroke through her silken hair with his fingers.

His laugh sounded softly behind her. 'What a long memory you have! Does that still rankle after all these years? I thought I had apologised for doing that.'

'Yes, but only because your mother made you.' She turned her head slowly to one side as the fingers of one of his hands found their way underneath her hair to the soft skin at her neck.

'Did she tell you?' He bent forward and rubbed his face in her hair, which surprised her into trembling.

'She was making sure that you did what she told you to do.' He pulled the sleek brown length aside and slid close to press his lips against the nape of her neck. His mouth was warm, and the light touch of his breath sent a delightful shiver down her back. She tried to wriggle away. 'Don't, Jason.'

He laughed again, his presence at her back immediate and palpable. 'That's what you used to say to me all the time. Couldn't you tell that the pranks were my way of showing that I liked you?'

'Good grief, with some of the things you pulled?' Her breath came short and fast, for some reason constricted in her throat.

He stood and then bent over to tuck his arms around her, one firmly around her shoulders while the other slid under her knees. Then with a gentle, easy movement, he straightened and headed out of the door, very careful not to knock her bandaged foot. She slid her arms around his neck, the skin sheathing that strong column warm against hers. As he strode through the upstairs hall, he replied drily, 'What did you expect me to do, send flowers? Come on, Robbie, I was just a kid.'

'Well, I don't care what you say. I think it was a pretty strange way of showing you liked me,' she grumbled. He went down the stairs lightly, and she could feel the fluidity of his working muscles, his lean gracefulness. At the moment she was too worn out and in too much pain, but later she was to flush darkly at the memory of the sensation.

In the living-room, Jason eased her on to the couch and then knelt on the floor close by, bringing his face down until his straight nose touched hers, grey eyes vivid with laughter and something else. He said softly, 'Aren't you glad I show that I like you in different ways now?'

That had her blinking rapidly and she grew hot as she tried to pull away, but he held her head still as he tilted his own sideways. Firm, full lips took hers as her eyes fell shut, and he kissed her lightly, teasingly before drawing away. She opened her eyes slowly and stared at him, both looking and feeling bowled over. His own lean, handsome expression lightened until he looked positively delighted. He stood and whipped away, a curiously excited, intense movement, and he called back over his broad shoulder, 'You should be starving. I'll go and make you something to eat, okay?'

'Okay,' she mumbled, but she was doubtful whether he had heard her or not as he was already striding purposefully down the hall. But she didn't bother repeating herself. She had the feeling that he wouldn't listen to her anyway.

He was soon back again, with a tray balanced carefully in his large, capable hands. The first whiff of spicy, aromatic coffee hit her like a sledgehammer. She had forgotten that she hadn't eaten supper the night before, and she was suddenly ravenously hungry. She fell on the plate of delicately seasoned scrambled eggs and toast which he had prepared, with an enthusiasm that caused a swift, amused grin to crease across his face. Only when her plate was neatly clean and her cup of coffee drained did she sit back with a sigh of relief. When she glanced up, she found that he had done nothing but sit and watch as she ate, slumped indolently in her father's favourite armchair.

'Want any more?' he asked. She tucked her bare

foot underneath her, the other leg stuck straight out, and she took in every detail of his appearance. His hands were laced and tucked behind his head, arms flexed back, and his long, muscular legs were stretched out in front of him, the faded denim of his jeans straining against his thighs and lean hips. His shirt was open several buttonholes at his throat, giving golden glimpses of his hair-sprinkled chest. Having seen him shirtless countless times before, she couldn't think why that brief bare expanse was so tantalising.

'Nothing more to eat, thanks,' she replied, though she couldn't help the look she threw to her empty cup.

His quick grey gaze caught it, and he straightened attentively in his chair. 'How about another cup of coffee?'

'I don't know,' she said longingly.

'Sure you do,' he told her impatiently. 'Yes, or no, do you want another cup?'

'Well, maybe if you had a cup . . .' she started, not looking at him.

'Yes or no!' he rapped out, startling her so much that she cried out, 'Yes!'

He rose to his feet and gave her a glowering look as he growled exasperatedly, 'Now, why on earth couldn't you have said that to begin with?'

Her eyes fell, and at that she wore such a truly miserable demeanour that Jason's face quivered between real irritation and gentleness for a moment before giving way to the milder expression. 'I don't want you to wait on me hand and foot,' she muttered, avoiding his gaze as she pleated the bottom hem of her shirt between her fingers.

'Robbie,' he said with great patience, 'it's a lousy cup of coffee. I'm not exactly breaking my back.'

'But this is your holiday,' she said, as if that explained everything. He looked more mystified than ever.

'What does that have to do with anything?' He was staring at her in puzzlement, and as her brown eyes lifted to meet his, they filled with unexpected tears, going liquidly brilliant, startling both herself and him. His expression reflected his shock, and then, realising she was taking the whole thing with utter seriousness, he dropped his impatient attitude and sat beside her on the couch.

She scrubbed angrily at her eyes with the backs of her knuckles and looked so much like the younger, defiant Robbie he'd known that he sighed heavily. 'You shouldn't be wasting your free time playing nursemaid to me!' she snapped with a surprising fierceness. 'Thank you very much. I've had enough. Go away.'

'But I don't want to go away,' he said with an odd little laugh. His hand landed lightly on her back, and he rubbed up and down. 'I want to stay and argue with you. Want to play a game of cards?'

'No.' Her tone was still truculent. The last thing in the world she wanted was for him to feel obligated into staying with her. She'd be glad if he left. At least then there would be some peace and quiet.

He sighed again at the stubborn, contrary angle of her jaw. 'All right. How about draughts?'

'No.'

'Scrabble. Chess. Anything in the world.' His voice was growing more and more fed up.

'No.'

'I suppose that covers it.' He stood and left the room. At first she couldn't believe it, but when she whipped her head around to look, he was gone.

She was all alone. Finally, at last. She hoped he would go and soak up some sun and enjoy himself. It was nice to have the house to herself. She bent her head and cried.

'My God!' Jason exploded at the sight of her. He was at the open archway that led into the hall, and if she'd had full use of both legs, she would have hit the ceiling. As it was, she jumped violently and whirled to see him striding quickly into the living-room, slapping down the two paperbacks he held. They landed on her TV tray, which wobbled on its unsteady legs. He came for her with such purpose gleaming out of his eyes that she shrank away from his touch.

But he wasn't about to let her go. He held her by the shoulders and shook her steadfastly until she shouted in outrage. She was quite a sight, her hair streaming like soft rain from her forehead, eyes full to overflowing with both her fury and her tears. He bent forward and eagerly, hotly, took her mouth.

Surprise had her lips soft and open. He bent her back to the couch and delved in deep with his tongue, tasting the warm wetness of her until she began to recover and she squirmed in protest. He was leisurely in pulling away, nibbling at the fullness of her lower lip so that she shook in response.

'You have some nerve,' she said in shaky belligerence.

He looked at her in horrified fascination as though he expected her to start raving at any moment. It was not a flattering look. 'What the hell is the matter with you, anyway?' he expostulated.

Robbie felt her composure going right out of the window, and she covered her face with her hands. The first sob she tried to repress, but it came out as an odd little snort. She was so mortified by that, she didn't even bother trying with the second, or third, or fourth sob that shuddered out. She made a supreme effort and managed to say almost calmly, 'I don't know.'

His hand came under her chin, and he forced her to look up at him. For the first time since they had begun the strangely upsetting conversation, there was the beginning of real anger darkening his eyes. 'Are you lying to me?'

She would have lied again, but his expression prompted her to second thoughts. 'Yes.'

Overcome at last, he let go of her and just sat there, slowly shaking his head. 'I will never understand you, Roberta Fisher. I will never, ever understand you.'

That stung, and she cried out, 'I only want you to go away and leave me alone! Can't you have a good enough holiday without tormenting me?'

His grey eyes widened as though she'd struck him, and then rage darkened his expression. She edged instinctively away at the sight. 'Me, tormenting you!' he shouted deeply, and literally surged to his feet. 'Come on, Robbie, let's be a little realistic here! What about the way you torment me? But that doesn't count, does it? I'm expected to handle that without saying a thing, aren't I?'

She gaped. Then she shook herself, and she closed her jaw with an audible click. Then she shrieked furiously, 'I have never tormented you in my life!'

He laughed sardonically, and started to pace the room. Then he snarled angrily, 'Go ahead, pull the other leg!'

Sudden, vivid memories came to mind of the way she used to get even with him for his horrid pranks, and she flushed dark red. 'I meant in recent years!' she snapped. Then in spite of herself, she ran her gaze down his lithely moving body and thought that she'd never seen such a handsome man.

Jason whirled to face her from the other end of the room. 'Damn it, girl, all you do is torment me!' he bellowed, and she clapped her hands over her ears. He was in front of her in three long steps, and he forcibly dragged her hands down. Then he leaned over her, his eyes two molten, shining pieces of silver. She stared up and found she couldn't look away. In a very soft, almost gentle voice that was infinitely worse than his shouting, he whispered, 'You have been tormenting me every night and every day this entire summer. You have been looking at every inch of my body with desire practically screaming from your big brown eyes. You respond eagerly whenever I kiss you, but when I try to touch or caress any other part of your body, you shy away as though I've done something unspeakably vile. It's coming to the point where I don't even know whether I'm coming or going anymore, and I ache so badly to make love to you, I can't sleep at night. Oh yes, cringe away! You want to tell me the truth about yourself and expect me to listen with patience, but you can't take it when I give you a little truth of my own!'

Her indrawn breath was a deeply racked, harsh sound. Her face crumpled, and her slim shoulders convulsed uncontrollably. The fury that so changed his face turned to self-condemnation, and he sat down abruptly to pull her against his chest. His head bent wearily over hers, and after a moment, he said quietly, 'I'm sorry. Ssh, Rob, don't. I'm sorry.'

Strange, when he had hurt her so, strange to find her hands curling urgently into the front of his shirt. Strange that she should feel so full of pain and yet so full of an overflowing comfort that stemmed from an inexhaustible source within him. Bittersweet. She never cried when arguing with anyone else, only Jason. Sometimes even then, she didn't understand why.

'It's my fault,' she said unsteadily, and she felt his head shake in negation. His heartbeat sounded loud against her ear and his arms enfolded her tightly, holding her against his body warmth. 'No, it is. I just have . . . have some things I need to work out.'

'I know. I know.'

'I only w-wanted you to stay if you wanted to. I wanted you to enjoy yourself. I had to go and sprain my damned ankle. I did want you to stay.'

'Robbie,' he murmured against her temple gently. 'The only reason I asked you to go to Cedar Point was so that we could spend the day together. I didn't care about the stupid amusement park. I care about you.'

She lifted her head to stare into his eyes. No longer were they filled with that frightening, alienating, hot anger, but instead they held a wry twisted look that was close to amusement, but not quite. She took a deep breath and opened her mouth. What she would have said, she hadn't a clue. What she would have said just then was quite lost, as the front doorbell suddenly, loudly, rang through the intimacy of their quiet, tired, open declarations, shattering the moment forever.

CHAPTER EIGHT

A SINGULARLY frustrated look entered Jason's eyes, and his softened expression hardened to bleak resignation. Robbie didn't see, for she was too busy scrubbing frantically at her damp, pink eyes and attempting to straighten her rumpled hair. The doorbell sounded again, and Jason rose in a quick, impatient movement to answer it.

Marilyn's voice came from the open doorway, but Robbie couldn't hear what she said. She heard Jason's reply clearly, though, as he said, 'Oh, she's sleeping right now. Yes, I'll tell her you stopped by. She'll be glad to have her bag back. I suppose her car is still in the restaurant parking lot? No, it won't be a problem. Her father and I can go and pick it up this evening when he gets home from work. Thank you, Marilyn. It's nice seeing you again, too. Take care.'

He shut the door again and walked slowly back into the living-room. When she glanced quickly up at him, she saw him turning her bag over and over in his hands while he stared down at it absently. There was a dampened spot on his shirt which had been made by her tears. After a moment, he raised his head and glanced at her, then he placed her bag carefully on a small table nearby. 'I thought you'd rather not see anyone right now,' he explained quietly.

He was quite right, of course. She moistened her dry lips and whispered, 'Thanks.'

His grey eyes fell to the forgotten TV tray. 'Did you still want another cup of coffee?' he asked.

Such a totally unimportant, stupid beginning to the argument: such an inauspicious way to let out festering tensions. Silently she shook her head.

Absently, he picked up the two books he had brought into the room, and handed them to her. 'I thought you might like to read, since you weren't interested in doing anything else.'

Those easy, baffling tears blinded her again, but she refused to let them spill over and blinked them back rapidly. She couldn't think what was the matter with her. She was acting quite unlike herself, and everything was affecting her in the oddest way. If this was what happened when one suffered an injury, like some sort of delayed shock, then she would certainly do her best to avoid having another one. 'Yes, I think I would.'

She noticed that he carefully avoided touching her fingers, and she found that it hurt incredibly. 'Well,' he said, with some show of briskness. 'I'd better clean up the mess I made in the kitchen. Will you be all right in here for a little while?'

No, she wouldn't. Something was terribly wrong with her, and she couldn't understand it. The balance of her world was upset, and she didn't know how to fix it. 'Sure,' she replied, eyes downbent. 'No problem.'

He moved, and she thought he seemed to sway towards her. But she must have been mistaken, for when she looked up quickly, he was bending over the tray to pick it up, and then he walked out of the room.

Left all alone, she felt achingly lonely. She

struggled to settle herself in a comfortable position on the couch, but her ankle throbbed abominably no matter what she did. She perused listlessly first one, then the other of the paperbacks that he had brought to her, flipping through the printed pages without reading a single word. She could hear the faint sounds of water running, along with the chink of china. What was Jason thinking? He had sounded almost as though he hated her when he finally lost his temper, and she couldn't blame him, for everything he had said was true. Her head fell back dejectedly against the pillow she'd tucked beneath her neck, and then her eyes closed wearily. What a mixed-up mess everything was. What a terrible, mixed-up mess.

She was sound asleep when Jason peered into the living-room a little later. After standing and regarding her pale, exhausted visage in contemplative silence, he gently took the book that rested on her stomach, eased it out from her slack fingers and then set it on the nearby table beside her bag. The other paperback was on the floor by the couch, and he bent to pick that up before walking over to the armchair and settling himself. His demeanour was that of a man prepared to wait for a long time. He opened the book and began to read.

She woke some time later, ruffled and bemused. Jason then carried her to the bathroom so that she could wash her face, straighten her appearance, and use the facilities. He made them a light snack for lunch at which she only picked, and they both treated each other with a delicate, painful wariness. They played cards throughout the remainder of the afternoon, Robbie's foot and ankle propped carefully on a cushioned chair, and soon she began to anticipate her father's arrival home.

'Oh, by the way,' said Jason, as he sprawled in his chair opposite hers at the dining table, 'Herb invited someone named Marjorie over for supper tonight. Do you know her?'

She perked up a little with pleasure. 'Oh, yes. She goes to the same church that he does, a lovely woman. I've been wondering when he'd find the courage to ask her over.'

'Yes, well, he thought you and I would be in Sandusky until late. Rather than have him cancel it, or have you forced to make an unwelcome third at supper tonight, I offered to take you over to my parents' place for the evening. Is that all right with you?'

She lifted her brown eyes from her hand of cards and met his, which were shuttered and unreadable. Her heart twisted at that. Forlornly she wished he could relax and be open and natural with her again, but she was beginning to wonder if that would ever be possible. She tried to smile normally. 'That's fine. What are you going to feed me?'

Her question prompted a slight, but genuine laugh from him, and her heartache eased. 'I'm not sure, exactly,' he replied and then tossed down his discard. She perused the upturned card with the beginnings of satisfaction. 'It depends on what's in the refrigerator. I might have to make a trip to the shops.'

'I refuse to touch anything over a week old,' she

informed him and picked up his discard to rearrange her hand and lay the entire thing out to his suddenly disgusted expression. 'Gin.'

When her father came home, he and Jason left immediately to pick up her Volvo while she fumed helplessly on the couch. She was beginning to feel better after her long night's sleep and mid-day nap, and she found herself extremely irritated by her enforced immobility. When Herb and Jason returned about twenty minutes later, they found her glowering dangerously into space, her un-usually volatile emotions rocketing back to the depths of depression.

Her father stopped just inside the living-room and nudged Jason's elbow as the younger man joined him. 'What's wrong with her?' he asked, more than loudly enough for her to hear. She ignored him determinedly.

'I think she's just had a frustrating day,' replied Jason in a confidential tone. 'Looks vicious, though, doesn't she?'

'Do you think she's upset that I have a date tonight and she's not invited?' continued Herb cautiously, edging towards his armchair while giving the couch and her a meticulously wide berth.

'That could be it,' said the younger man thoughtfully. 'Of course, it might just be her own, sweet disposition that's prompted this . . .'

'Oh, for God's sake!' Robbie exploded, and her annoyance was so great that she threw her couch pillow at Jason, who laughingly ducked out of harm's way. He went to retrieve the pillow while she glared at her father, realised the two had been trying to get just such a response out of her, and subsided into grumbling under her breath.

Jason then swooped down on her, heaved her up into his arms, and strode to the front door. 'You'll be pleased to know that I picked up something edible at the shops for our supper,' he said sweetly, while she peered bobbingly over his shoulder at her father, who was wearing a pleased, vacant smile. 'Now, since I have my hands full, open the door and say good night, Robbie.'

She glanced up briefly at twinkling, warm grey eyes, turned to twist the doorknob and thrust it open, and carolled, 'Have a nice evening with Marjorie, and good night, Robbie!'

Herb laughingly echoed the farewell, and Jason slipped sideways through the doorway with her. Then her self-consciousness was brief but intense as he carried her across the lawn. Fortunately the street and their cul-de-sac were empty, and they were soon inside the Morrows' house, which was much the same as it had ever been, though she hadn't been inside for a surprisingly long time.

'Where do you want to sit, in front of the television or in the kitchen while I start our supper?' Jason asked her. She had her arms wound around his neck and was held tightly against his chest. Though she was not exactly small or lightweight, he didn't seem to have any apparent problem with carting her around indefinitely.

'If you're very good, I'll keep you company,' she told him grudgingly, to which he immediately started for the family-room. 'No, no! I take it back!' she cried laughingly then, tightening her arms around him.

His face turned towards her, and his close, grey eyes sparkled with delight. 'Why, Robbie,' he said lightly. 'If you hold on any tighter, I might believe that you care after all. Is that a blush I see darkening your little cheeks?'

She muttered fulminatingly as she fought the urge to squirm, 'Just put me down, will you?' Obediently he went down on one knee and sat her on the floor in the hall. At that she looked around her, sighed, and said very patiently, 'I didn't mean here, you simpleton.'

He straightened and laughed down at her. 'Of course you didn't,' he said cheerfully, and headed for the kitchen.

He never ceased to amaze her. At every turn he was a different person, and she struggled to conform her perception of him with every shift in mood. He was her brother, stranger, friend and lover. He was everything and nothing. A disturbing little voice whispered inside her mind as though coming from another person. It reminded her that Jason wasn't her lover yet. Not quite yet. And what was she to him?

'Sometimes teasing you can be no fun at all,' he complained from her right, and she turned to see him leaning against the doorway to the kitchen, arms crossed over his chest, one leg kicked over the other. He tilted his golden-brown head at her, like a bright-eyed bird. 'Aren't you going to say something nasty?' was his next hopeful question. 'Maybe mutter a few curses, throw a temper tantrum, do anything at all?'

'Nope. I wouldn't give you the satisfaction.' She bumped over to the wall on her rear and leaned against the side with one hand as she rose to her good foot. Then, arms flapping like an ungainly, landbound bird, she hopped precariously towards the kitchen, and he shot off the doorpost to catch her by the waist, laughingly.

'Hold on a moment! The last thing we need is for you to sprain the other ankle. Put your arm around my waist—ouch! What was that pinch for, you little fiend?'

'For leaving me in the hallway, what else?'

He saw her settled comfortably in a kitchen chair and then neatly, quickly set their supper cooking on the stove. For simple items like her scrambled eggs, he didn't do badly, but Jason had never been a cook by any stretch of the imagination. What he had picked up for their evening meal was a few frozen gourmet dinners which had become so popular across America. She knew better than to complain. She and Herb frequently indulged in the prepared dinners, and so she knew from experience that they were far better than anything she could hope to get from Jason.

While the plastic packets bubbled in boiling water on the stove, they sat and talked quietly. Soon the meal was ready to serve, and to her pleasant surprise he produced a chilled bottle of wine. The evening went quite well, their earlier wariness having dissolved under the weight of their long friendship.

She had been screwing up her courage to speak of their earlier argument throughout the entire meal, her eyes periodically searching Jason's relaxed, lean face across the table from her. He seemed quite normal, and yet there was a slight, almost indefinable difference in the way he treated her. He repeatedly, delicately and politely avoided any physical contact with her, apart from what was strictly necessary and she was amazed at how that troubled her.

She watched him pour more wine into their glasses, her mind preoccupied with the struggle to speak plainly, and she blurted out, 'You know I'm a virgin, don't you?'

The bottle-neck which was resting lightly against the rim of her glass, jerked spasmodically and wine spilled all over the table. Jason swore explosively, crashed the bottle to the table in a savage movement that made her jump, and then put his elbows on the table's surface and buried his face in his hands. Feeling hot and miserable under the pressure of her own intense embarrassment, not comprehending his reaction, Robbie stared down at her hands as she twisted them together in her lap.

'How many times,' said Jason, too carefully, 'do I have to tell you, not to startle me so when I'm doing something.'

'You weren't drinking anything!' she snapped back and fell silent. She looked up to find Jason peering wearily over one hand which still covered the lower half of his face.

'I certainly hope you don't think that there's anything wrong with virginity,' he said with some difficulty. She could only surmise that he felt as embarrassed by her own gauche way of beginning the subject as she did, and she became even more mortified.

Urgently reaching for her glass, she gulped down what little wine he had managed to pour into it. Then she looked away blindly and muttered, 'I don't know. It's so complicated. It's just not something you confess right off the bat. "Oh, hi. I'm a virgin." '

She didn't see his broad shoulders shake convulsively, but she thought his voice sounded peculiarly strangled as he agreed, 'No, I know exactly what you mean.'

'I mean, so many people aren't these days.'

'A startling amount, I should think.'

Her brown gaze flashed quickly to his face, and her cheeks went dark red with sudden hurt. 'You're laughing at me!' she accused heatedly.

'No, no,' he hastened to reply. 'I'm laughing with you.'

'How the hell can that be?' she cried furiously. 'I don't think it's very funny!' Her hands slapped the surface of the table in outrage.

He reached quickly for one of her hands, but she jerked them back to her lap and his landed in the spilled wine. Shaking them absently, he insisted, 'I'm not laughing at your expense, damn it. I'm as sympathetic as I can be. I happen to think that too much is made of sexual affairs. They're vastly overrated. Any animal can couple. It's the love shared between two people that matters, otherwise it's just a biological function.'

'Biological function,' she snorted miserably, and bowed her head to rub at her eyes. It had been a stupid thing for her to confess in the first place, and the strain of the conversation was giving her a terrible headache. 'Somehow that makes it sound so easy. But it's not.'

'Robbie,' he said gently, looking as strained as she felt, 'it's only easy when it's shallow. Your friend Casey's taken the easy way out.' A long pause, while she listened to the distant sounds of a passing motorcycle. Somewhere in the fading light of evening a buzz-saw whined. When he spoke again, his voice was quite low, 'Why are you telling me this?'

'Because,' she whispered, 'I didn't want you to think that I was playing some kind of game with you. And I didn't want you to think that I thought your touch was vile.'

She glanced up unexpectedly. His light eyes were blazing hot and bright with some kind of deep emotion, and his face was tightly clenched to contain it all. The mellow overhead lighting threw strong slanting shadows over his face, emphasising the cut of his cheekbones, the fullness of his lower lip, the length of his lashes. 'It's one of the bravest, most generous gestures I've seen you make,' he replied, gentle affection strong and palpable in his voice. The uncomfortable, tight feeling eased in her chest and she was able to relax.

'I'd been bracing myself to tell you all evening,' she confessed further, giving him a funny, twisted little smile. 'But it surprised me, too, when it popped out like it did.'

But Jason didn't return her smile. Instead, he looked even more strained. He thrust himself from his chair and walked away from the table while she stared blankly after him and wondered if he meant to leave her alone. But he stopped in front of the refrigerator and bowed his head. Strangely, to her mind, he seemed uncertain. She had seen him many ways, gentle, diffident, sensitive, angry and belligerent, but rarely had she ever seen him uncertain. 'I'm glad you told me,' he said finally and thrust his hands into his pockets. 'You see, it makes it a little easier for me to confess something to you.'

A thousand different possibilities ran through her mind at that moment. She was scared. She was so scared, her heart started to pound and her lips began to quiver. He was going to say that he no longer wanted her now that he knew. He was going to confess the number of women he'd been with. She didn't know what he was going to confess, but one thing was certain, she soon found out. She would never have guessed it in a million years.

CHAPTER NINE

JASON turned back to face her. His expression was pale, guarded, and his eyes met hers as he told her quietly, 'I, too, am a virgin.'

The shock stayed with her for days.

She had expected one of two scenarios. Either Jason would have twinges of conscience because she was sexually innocent and so he would leave her be, or he would sweep her tenderly into his arms and reassure her that everything was all right because he had enough experience for both of them. But she should have known she would have no such luck. Real life never was that simple.

By Sunday she was able to hobble around on her own. She was careful not to put too much strain on her ankle, which was remarkably slow to loosen up. Her days were filled with late mornings, lazy, sunshine-filled afternoons, and quiet evenings spent reading or watching television with her father and Jason.

Those were the activities that occupied her time, but the subject that occupied her thoughts was Jason. She couldn't stop thinking about him. He was such an enigma. Certainly, he had more than enough money and the time to take a holiday anywhere he wished, and yet he stayed at home doing nothing in particular, lazing his days away in much the same way as she was. Instead of keeping his virginity a secret as most males would have, he had chosen to tell her the truth. After confessing his deep attraction to her, he seemed perfectly content to fall back on the rules of their old platonic friendship. The waiting, disturbing shadow in the night had disappeared.

He was driving her crazy.

She continued to watch him helplessly. He always seemed to be practically naked, his long, sleek muscular limbs bare and glistening with a light sheen of sweat in the summer heat. She remembered the frustrated and intense light in his grey eyes as he confessed his desire for her. She remembered the eager, excited way he had taken her mouth, the tension that had vibrated through his entire body.

She thought she understood now. He was a normal male in every way. That he had retained his virginity throughout college was nothing short of a miracle to her. He was good-looking, physically very attractive, intelligent, and certainly more sophisticated and mature in his outlook of the world than she was. What he was experiencing now was probably the intense, almost over-whelming, belated urge to indulge in his own sexuality.

That plunged her still strangely unstable emotions to the depths of depression. She should feel flattered and touched that he would want her of all people. She'd heard it said that a man always remembered his first woman. There was simply no doubt, her reaction was as incomprehensible to her as his actions were.

Jason joined her that Sunday afternoon and they talked desultorily while lazing in the sun.

When he excused himself later on, she murmured languidly, 'Want to come over for supper?'

She thought he hesitated as he stood squinting up at the sun. 'Thanks, but I'm going out tonight,' he replied finally.

Her heart gave an unpleasant jolt. She fervently hoped her face didn't reveal her inner reaction and stirred restlessly on her lounge chair. 'Oh?' she asked, studiously, falsely uninterested. 'Who's the lucky girl?'

He turned and met her gaze, his bright grey eyes standing out against the golden tan which had deepened several shades in the last week. They were far too observant, his eyes. 'Linda.'

The queer jerk in her chest had subsided to a dull ache, and she unconsciously put her hand under her breast in wonder at her physical response to his reply. She slid her glance down the taut, youthful vitality of his body and then looked away, holding her expression in tight control. 'So you managed to catch her when she wasn't seeing Ian, hm?'

Unseen by her, a look of weary anger quivered across his features, and he said shortly, 'Actually, she called me.'

He was already walking away when she jerked around to stare at him. She looked and felt quite stricken.

The evening passed by as slowly as if it were a thousand years. Robbie slouched on the couch and answered any comments from her father in monosyllabic replies. Jason pulled out of his driveway at five-forty-six, the rust-coloured sports car gleaming clean and bright as it purred down the street. She knew the precise time. She'd been watching out of the front window.

Herb went to bed quite early as he had to work in the morning, and Robbie sat watching television programme after programme without taking any of it in. Her gaze strayed out of the window more and more as ten o'clock rolled by. She bit her nails. She fidgeted impatiently with her ankle bandage.

When midnight came, she finally rose from the couch and flipped off all the downstairs lights. There was no way anyone would be able to accuse her of waiting up until Jason got home. She would go upstairs and wait in darkness by her bedroom window.

When his car pulled into the cul-de-sac, headlights glaring, it was nearly two in the morning. Robbie sat curled into a compact bundle in a chair beside her window, staring dry-eyed into the shadowed night. The dull chest-ache had died away long ago to a leaden, heavy feeling. Jason climbed out of his car, and with her window open she heard the slam of his door clearly. If she leaned her forehead against the wire screen, she could just make out his tall, blurred figure as he stood in his driveway. Her heart leaped and started an excited, frantic pounding. He turned and walked noiselessly across the lawn towards her house. But he stopped some distance away and stood still for a long, long moment before turning to walk back to his parents' house. After watching until he disappeared from her sight, Robbie sat for several minutes just staring at the opposite wall until she finally stirred and dragged herself to bed, refusing to acknowledge that her original excitement had given way to a bitter disappointment.

By morning, after a sleepless night, she had come to a decision, and she called her doctor's office for an appointment early in the day. Luck was with her for she had caught his office on a slow day, and she drove herself to the appointment gingerly, as it was the first time she had gone out since she had sprained her ankle. She was back home again by ten, her complexion pale, her expression set.

After pulling her car into the garage, she limped through the downstairs of the house absently, for once not even noticing her ungraceful stride. She threw off her skirt and blouse upstairs and slipped on her usual shorts and summer top while wondering uncertainly if she was doing the right thing. Her handbag sat on her dresser and inside was tucked her purchase from the doctor.

The conflict inside her had wearied her so that she had to give in to her longings. She couldn't look ahead. She didn't know what she expected in her life any more. All she knew was that she wanted Jason more than anything else. She wanted to give and take a most precious gift with him, to share that first experience beyond all doubts and uncertainties, and she would have taken whatever consequences came her way.

Last night had shaken her badly. She had realised with a sharp suddenness that she had fallen into taking Jason's presence for granted, as she had throughout their childhood. But Jason had left her once and gone away, showing her that such thinking was dangerously false. They both had separate working spheres, relationships and experiences to go through, different life decisions to make.

Having seen the brunette only once and never having met her, she could view Linda only as a woman whose looks far outshone her own, not as a personality to be liked or disliked. There were a lot of Lindas in the world who would be more than willing to share an adult, caring relationship with Jason. If he wanted her, he wouldn't wait forever.

Having made such a momentous decision, Robbie fell into a quiet waiting attitude. For the life of her, she couldn't and wouldn't set up a seduction scene. She didn't know how to seduce, and she refused to act so falsely with someone who knew her so well.

Quietly she busied herself with light housework and settled into her father's armchair when her ankle began to hurt. The day trickled by far too slowly; she hadn't realised how much she needed to work until she was forced to do without it. Outside, quite close, she could hear a lawnmower kicking to life, and she limped to the window to see Jason working in his parents' front lawn in faded shorts and tennis shoes. His naked, golden back flexed with the strenuous exercise, the long, powerful leg muscles rippling sinuously with each swift stride.

About forty minutes later she heard the mower's engine die, and impulsively she walked out of the back door to cross over the fence and knock on his.

The next moment it was thrown open. Jason stood in the shadows of the house, a damp towel in his hand. 'Good morning,' he said, stepping back to let her enter. 'How's the ankle?'

'Better, thanks.' She came into the kitchen and looked around absently. She had always liked the colour scheme of greens and golds, and with a rich patterned tile setting off the décor nicely, the Morrows' kitchen was a pleasant place to be. Jason's grey eyes searched her face and figure questioningly while he rubbed his hot face and neck with the towel. She glanced at him quickly and tried to smile naturally. 'Not much of your holiday left now.'

He dropped the towel on to a chair and replied cheerfully, 'That's right, only a week left and I haven't done a blessed thing.'

'You should have taken a trip somewhere,' said Robbie, for that was what she would have done.

He shrugged and met her gaze with a curious smile. 'I suppose I needed to learn to appreciate the home life more.'

Silence fell and stretched out between them. She bent her head and traced a pattern on the nearby counter, trying very hard to think of something to say without asking the burning question that preyed upon her mind. She longed to ask about his night with Linda but couldn't bear to expose herself. Jason, that curious smile still curving his lips, circled the kitchen table slowly and approached. She pretended not to notice, but every muscle in her body screamed with awareness of him.

He stopped just beside her and reached up with one warm hand to touch at her hair, her neck. 'Something on your mind, Rob?' he asked softly.

'I just wanted to know if you'd like to come over for supper since you were busy last night,' she said all in a rush, the thought having just occurred to her.

He moved closer. 'Ah, yes. Last night. Did you think of me?' He was right at her back, and he bent his head to nuzzle lightly in her hair. She quivered at the sensation and her head felt suddenly too heavy to keep upright, falling back to his shoulder. She felt his hands, hard and heavy, on her waist and he slid them around to her flat stomach. Her heartbeat was going completely crazy, wildly, erratically thumping against the wall of her chest like a bird attempting to escape.

She said weakly, 'I don't know what you mean.'

That made him laugh. 'Maybe you don't at that.' His hands slid up in a long, slow, smooth motion that had her whole body trembling, as he cupped her breasts. She made a sound and flushed hot, her mind racing in disconcerted circles. The only thing she understood was that he had broken through his intention to treat her platonically, and it sent her to a near panic.

The whole caress couldn't have lasted more than a few moments. In the next instant everything had changed, and suddenly he gripped her roughly by the hipbones and held her tightly back against him, his mouth driving hungrily down to trace the angle of her jaw, the line of her neck. She felt his lips tremble. His body was hard, rock-hard, tense and hot and eager. Her hand came up and she touched his brow, his cheekbone, sliding up to cup the back of his head.

Then he took her by the shoulders and held her

between his hands until she thought he might snap her in two. His strong arms shook with effort, and suddenly he pushed her away from him in a violent movement. She stumbled in shock, and then whirled to face him. His head was hanging low, his lips bloodless over clenched teeth, his hands gripping the edge of the counter so that the knuckles showed red and white,

'Get out of here,' he whispered.

That hurt. She licked her dry lips and asked quaveringly, 'But what's wrong?' There was a dark, mottled flush across his cheekbones, and a muscle jerked spasmodically in his jaw. He was a stranger, a clenched, dangerous stranger.

'Just get out.'

Earlier she would have. She was confronted once again by the unknown in him. But she was tired of inexplicabilities and the unknown. Though she was honestly unsure of what he would do, she drew close to his side and put her hand on his bare, rigid shoulder. He drew in a harsh, deep breath. 'I don't understand. Talk to me.'

'You fool,' he rasped. 'I can't take much more of this. Don't you understand what touching you and yet not making love is doing to me? I was about to rip off your clothes.'

She flinched violently at his bald statement, which sent a dark look of self-mockery twisting his features. Never in all her imaginings had she comprehended actual, immediate reality. This was the real moment of decision, not when she had so easily made the trip to the doctor's. She had never made love before and all her senses told her that here was a male animal barely held in check. But this was Jason. Her hand slid down his back in a long stroke, and he closed his eyes and swallowed hard.

'If you'd give me just a moment, I could take them off instead,' she whispered.

It took a moment for the enormity of what she had suggested to sink in. His head snapped up, and he stared at her with dilated eyes, flaring nostrils. One hand left the counter to cup her cheek. His voice shook. 'Robbie——'

There was a look of naked apprehension in her eyes. He pulled away from the counter to take her gently into his arms. Suddenly her fear dissolved at the human touch, and she held on to him for a long, wordless hug. She knew him again.

He breathed as though labouring under some kind of physical strain. A film of sweat broke out over his slim, powerfully taut body. She sensed something seeming to snap inside him, a long-checked emotion released, an overwhelming urge unleashed. He pulled her face up to his and ravished her lips so that she felt almost as though she were being eaten alive. His hungry passion ignited hers, and she held the back of his head with trembling hands. Then he picked her up and strode quickly through the house to his bedroom, his expression full of such raw purpose that she had to hide her face in his neck.

He laid her on his bed tenderly. Her emotions and senses were heightened to a fever-pitch. Her eyes overflowed with tears at the reverent way he stroked her slight breasts. At that, he bent over her and kissed her lips, her wet cheeks, her eyes. Her hands ran over his body with greediness, touching his thighs, his flat stomach, his shoulders. They undressed in the shadowed, summer-warmed room and took each other's virginity with at first painful, touching awkwardness and then hot, eager excitement. It was the most profound moment she'd ever experienced, and afterward she held his head to her breast. His sobbing, panting breath eased, and his body-sweat, which had seared her to the core, gradually cooled. Then she knew that he, too, had found the experience profound, for a few tickling wet drops slid sneakily down the side of her ribcage. This, from someone whom she had never known to cry in his life.

By unspoken, mutual consent, they went through the rest of the day with an appearance of normality. It was a thin veneer, however, and she thought the changes in both herself and Jason must be screamingly obvious to even the most casual of observers, though Herb didn't appear to notice a thing. Jason treated her with a deep, tender consideration, and whenever she found his eyes on her, they were filled with a light she'd never seen from him before. In turn, she was oddly exhausted and languidly, intensely, sensually aware of his every movement. Every part of his body was beautiful, filled with a fluidity that was sheer male grace.

Late the next morning, her doorbell rang and she strode to answer it with an increasingly graceful movement of her own. Her ankle was much better and she could move it almost as freely as she could before she had sprained it.

She threw the door wide open and then stared without moving, for several long moments at the uniformed man in front of her. She wasn't able to look straight at him, though, for he was obscured by the huge, ribboned box he held. 'Roberta Fisher?' he asked.

'Yes, that's me,' she said, ungrammatically. He thrust a clip-board into her hands.

'Sign, please.' She complied bemusedly, and he gave her the box in exchange for the clip-board and flashed her a toothy grin. 'Have a good day.'

She murmured something in reply and then slammed the door shut and raced for the couch where she tore off the ribbon and box-top to stare down amazedly at the largest bunch of long-stemmed red roses she'd ever seen. 'Oh, my,' she said weakly to the empty room. Nobody had ever sent her roses before. She started to count them, remembered she hadn't looked for a card, and searched the thin green wrapping paper. There was none. She went back to her counting and found three-dozen flowers nestling in the huge box.

Jason had left her last night after Herb had gone to bed, giving her a long, wordless look, a gentle kiss and a smile. There had been a strange significance in his gaze, and the memory of it came to her as she stared at her roses, a sweet, luscious scent filling the living-room.

She stood hurriedly and rushed out of the door with the box held tightly against her chest, and the next moment found her pounding with one fist at the Morrows' back door. Jason answered it a few moments later.

She stood and stared at him with her large brown eyes gone soft and liquid. In her bright casual clothes, she looked vibrant and healthy, long sleek limbs bare and dark to the summer heat. Her hair was gathered into a simple ponytail from which a few silken wisps had escaped to frame her thin face, and she was shyly, delightedly peering over the flower box at him with her arms around it as if she would never put it down.

After a long look, he smiled slowly, 'Why, Robbie,' said he, lightly innocent. 'What have you got there?'

She came into the house, set the box down with a plunk, and whirled. 'You sent them,' she accused with pleasure. Then as he lifted his brows, her shoulders began to droop. 'Didn't you?'

He laughed softly and to her the sound seemed to hold a deeper, more mellow and contented quality than it had before. As he confessed, she couldn't resist throwing her arms around his neck and bestowing a hearty kiss on his cheek.

His arms slid around her and held her close. She was flush against his lean, hard body and the pleasure that it brought her was surprisingly intense. She was unprepared for the yearning desire that swept through her body, and she raised heavy-lidded eyes to his face. He wore a curiously intent, bright expression, and slowly he brought down his parted lips. Her breath came short and restricted, and she raised her mouth eagerly for his fierce kiss.

Then his head reared back and he ran his glittering gaze over her facial features. He looked as stunned as she felt. 'My God,' he breathed slowly, 'how I want you.'

She leaned back against his arms and traced the

curve of his collarbone lightly with her fingertips.
A rushing, heady feeling of excitement ran through
her at the hot tension in his body. He took her by
the hand and led her to his room, where they
drank deeply from each other and made love with
a wild abandon.

Languid warmth filled her body, and she
couldn't keep her eyes open under the heavy
weight of her lids. Jason's heart was hammering
hard and fast in his chest as he lay beside her, and
she curled up close, one hand laid palm flat
against the silken hair and skin of his body in an
unconscious, but singularly possessive gesture. She
fell deeply asleep.

After a long time, Jason rose up on one elbow
and stared down at Robbie's sleeping face.
Feather-light, he drew a half circle from her brow,
to her temple, where her pulse beat against thin
skin, and then down to the precise cut of her upper
lip. She moved at the tickling sensation and
murmured, then settled again, her sleep unbroken.
There was something blind about that deep rest of
hers, her eyes closed and unseeing, her expression
softened like that of a young child's.

He lay back and stared up at the ceiling, the
grey of his eyes now smoky with an ebbing ember.
The bedcovers were kicked to the floor in the
warmth of the afternoon, but Robbie shivered as
though chilled and instinctively drew near to his
body length. He slid his arm under her head and
she nestled her cheek into his shoulder, so while
she slept, he held her, though his own eyes didn't
close and his mind took paths that only he could
see.

Later she woke up alone. For long moments she just lay in the strange bed and felt the heaviness in her limbs. Lovemaking had a curious way of sapping her energy, and though she had done nothing else physically strenuous that day, she felt exhausted. She stretched, felt the faint friction of her ankle bandage against smooth sheet and the soreness of her muscles, and she had to smile at the memory of Jason's gentle consideration which was so at odds with his powerful, surging passion. He must be somewhere in the house or garden.

Then a frown began to wrinkle her forehead, and she rolled to her side to curl up as though protectively shielding herself from something. The actual realisation dawned on her. She was having an affair. The word instantly brought images of others whom she knew indulged in affairs, and Casey from the restaurant immediately came to mind. Robbie winced and shied away from the comparison. It wasn't the same thing at all. She was making love to Jason, a lifelong friend. Theirs was a relationship of ... of ... well, at the moment, she wasn't sure what their relationship was. But it had certainly endured a lot, and it wasn't as if she were promiscuous.

She resolved to dismiss the whole thing from her mind for the time being, and she rose to go to the bathroom down the hall and shower quickly. It felt rather odd to be showering in a strange bathroom just next-door to her house and the shower she had used now for twelve years. That thought began to bother her, too, niggling at the back of her mind as she wondered what Jason's parents were doing that day. Most likely they were basking in the Greek Isles and thinking of home. How would they feel if they knew about her and Jason? More unsettling, how would her father feel?

The first seeds of doubt had been well sown.

Wrapped in a towel, she hurried back to Jason's room and dressed. Then she used his hairbrush to pull back her brown length into another ponytail. When she went searching for Jason, she found him in the back garden, whistling cheerfully as he hung several pairs of jeans and shorts out to dry. She looked out of the back window for some time, absently admiring the play of rippling muscles across his naked back. A quick flush tinged her cheeks as she thought of how she had so-urgently gripped that broad male back, just a few hours ago.

She glanced back, saw her roses again, still in their box on the kitchen table, and she had to smile again at the fragrant scent that reached her even from that distance. With a quick stride, she gathered them up and slipped out of the back door, heading for her lawn as she called out, 'Coming over for supper tonight?'

He threw her a warm smile over his shoulder and removed two clothes-pegs from his mouth to reply, 'I'm not sure. Some time this afternoon I'd meant to run over to my apartment and check up on things, but time got away from me.' That with a wicked, white grin. 'Maybe I'd better not, but I promise to pop by later on, if you'd like.'

'Sure.' She flashed him a responding smile and turned to go, but he ran over to her and tilted her head up for a long, slow, lazy kiss. Then, after staring laughingly down into her flustered expression, he let her go and went back to his work.

Robbie went inside and rummaged in the kitchen cupboards for something in which to put her flowers. She had to use three vases, one of which she put in her bedroom, the other two she put downstairs. She didn't know how she was going to explain them to her father. She pondered that logistical problem as she began making supper.

The phone rang, and she hurried to answer it. With an inordinate amount of surprise, she greeted Ian. He sounded peculiarly short and grim as he asked her out for a drink that evening.

'No, I can't make it,' she replied slowly, unwilling to see him. 'I'm busy. Look, is anything wrong? You sound upset.'

He was immediately, painfully hearty. 'Good grief, no! I've just had a lousy day at work and wanted some company. Well if not tonight, maybe we can get together this weekend, how's that?'

'Why don't you give me a call in a few days?' she prevaricated, finding herself unable to give him a second rejection in a row in light of his obviously low mood. 'We can talk about it later when I have more idea of what my schedule will be like.'

They rang off and Robbie went back to her cooking in a thoughtful frame of mind. It was strange how her dating days with Ian seemed like another era when they had literally been a matter of days. She felt as though she had changed that much. She wasn't sure how she had changed, for the depth of her new range of emotions was so vast she had only just begun to explore them, but she was sure that she would never be the same again.

After tucking a roast chicken into the oven and putting potatoes on the stove to boil, she wandered into the living-room and threw herself on to the couch. Her father would be home at any minute now and she still had to think of something semi-plausible to tell him about her lovely roses.

A car pulled into the off-shooting pavement that was their small cul-de-sac, and she glanced out of the window idly. It wasn't her father's car, nor was it Jason's or their other neighbour's, and her interest quickened slightly as she watched to see whose driveway it would pull into.

The car purred into the Morrows' driveway, and curiously she watched the driver step out. The late afternoon sun caught a gleaming, raven-dark head, and Robbie felt an odd, sluggish shock as she watched Jason's friend Linda, looking stunningly beautiful, straighten to look around her.

Jason must have also heard the car approach, for he came out of the front door and approached the brunette, who turned and walked straight into his arms. That shook her. That really shook her, for Jason's golden-brown head came down to rest atop Linda's for a brief moment, before he gently urged her into the house and shut the door behind them.

It didn't necessarily mean anything. There could have been a thousand different reasons for her to visit him, and for him to receive her in such a tenderly caring way. Robbie told herself that fiercely over and over again, while desperately trying to dampen down the sick feeling of hot jealousy that choked her throat.

Herb walked through the front door a few minutes later and Robbie put on her normal, cheerful expression. When he saw the flowers, he naturally asked where she had got them from. She was so preoccupied with her jealousy and harsh effort to appear normal that she told him the plain truth. That sent his eyebrows shooting up in surprise, but she didn't even notice.

Supper tasted like sawdust, though her father complimented her several times. Television couldn't hold her attention. Later on, Jason phoned briefly to tell them that he wouldn't be over that evening, and Herb took the call.

CHAPTER TEN

WHEN the travel-agent had suggested the Virgin Islands for a holiday, courtesy of a late reservation cancellation, Robbie had leaped at the idea. She had only wanted to get away to think, to put Cincinnati and home far away in a desperate bid to get her life into perspective. Anywhere would have been fine.

For the first of the two weeks, she had thrown herself into a feverish schedule of sightseeing on the island St Croix. She swam hard in the afternoons and was still going strong in the evenings when she watched the nightclub entertainment. She thoroughly explored Fredericksted, the city where she was staying, and she joined any available tours. She grew even darker after lying whole afternoons in the hot southern sun and struck up several holiday friendships.

A surprising number of men, both young and old, had made advances that ranged from the utterly suave to the rather unsettling, and the downright pathetic. She went out once or twice, but they always seemed to have the same goal in mind and were frantic to get her into bed before the end of their holidays. After a while, she thought she should carry a stop-watch around with her to time each carefully executed manoeuvre.

To each and every one, she gave a firm and emphatic refusal. Somehow the thought of getting physically intimate with a man after the special experience she had shared with Jason was completely repelling to her. That was a scary realisation.

But then everything about Jason scared the sin out of her. Every single thing about him. She had become obsessed with him. She dreamed and thought about him, she yearned, she mooned, she sighed. But somehow she would have to get over her infatuation for him and settle down to leading her life again. He was messing up her mind so that she couldn't think properly. She had to keep reminding herself of their differences. She should never have made love with him, never, never.

The second week, her nervous energy was spent, and she drooped, either on the beach, in the hotel lounge, or in her room. Her ankle had swelled a few times when she had been excessive in her walking about the city, and so she pampered it. She slept late as was her usual custom and sometimes took naps. The two-week leave of absence she had taken from work simply wasn't going to be enough.

She was going home tomorrow and she still hadn't resolved a thing. She was no closer to working out her feelings and fears than she had been when she came, and she didn't know what she was going to do or say when she saw Jason again.

She hadn't told him when she was leaving, and that was part of the complication. She didn't know what he would do or how he had reacted when Herb had informed him that she had left. She didn't know whether she should expect rage or cheerful indifference, and she found that she was equally afraid of both. The day after he had spent the evening with Linda, she had simply gone downtown to make travel arrangements, fallen into an extraordinary piece of luck with the cancelled reservation, and had left that very evening.

Robbie stretched and yawned as she lay sprawled on her beach towel. The sand was hard under her stomach, and she had to pound out a few bumps that dug into her hip-bone. The sun was a fierce, relentless glow. She hadn't thought it possible, but the day after she had first spent the afternoon in the tropical sun, her skin had been tender to the touch and she had just finished a light peeling, though no red had shown through the deep brown of her tan.

'Hello,' said a strange, male voice from directly above her, and a shadow fell across her head and shoulders. With a deep sigh, she hid her face in her crossed arms for a moment before coolly replying to the greeting. 'Mind if I join you?' he asked.

She lifted her brown, sun-streaked head and saw a black shadow surrounded by blinding white sun rays, and she said briefly, 'Help yourself, if you're not a chatterer and you're not trying to pick me up. I've had my fill of that, and I'm in no mood to tolerate any nonsense.'

It was remarkable, she mused sleepily, what a put-off brisk annoyance really could be. The fellow looked around him with a great show of nonchalance, muttered something to her which she didn't catch, and set off for easier prey.

That evening, as she had for the last two weeks, she dined excellently and savoured every bite. The holiday had made a huge dent in her savings account, but it was something she'd always

promised herself. She wished she could have
appreciated it more than she had. After the meal,
she strayed into the bar for a drink and to listen to
the music, but after she had been forced to give a
few sharp rebuffs to a man who was distinctly
unsteady on his feet, she went to her room and
locked the door behind her with the feeling of
having escaped from a jungle. Any other time she
would have felt flattered at the attention, but she
was simply too preoccupied for that sort of thing.

She called her father to let him know what time
her flight would be in the next day. After a wait,
her phone-call went through, and Herb sounded
delighted through the slight crackle of the overseas
connection. 'Hello, honey! This is an unexpected
pleasure. Is everything all right? Are you having a
good time?'

'Yes, everything's fine, and I've had a wonderful
time,' she assured him cheerfully, if not very
truthfully. 'If you can believe it, I got sunburn on
my first day at the beach. How's everything there?'

'Just fine. I've had Marjorie over several times,
and the house is a mess,' he chuckled. 'Not that
the two have anything to do with each other. Are
you sure you can afford this phone-call?'

'Don't worry about the money,' she dismissed
lightly. 'I just wanted to call and let you know that
my flight will be arriving tomorrow evening at six-
thirty, and I was wondering if you could pick me
up at the airport.'

'Sure, no problem. Which airline are you flying
on?' She told him, and then she started to make
appropriate closing noises when he interrupted
quickly with, 'Listen, Jason's sitting right here,

would you like to talk to him before you hang up?'

Foolishly, her heart leaped with the unexpected shock of hearing Jason's name. Talking to her father and discussing Jason was bringing them both as close as though they were in the next room, and the whole purpose of her holiday was shattered into indiscernible fragments. She replied, too fast, 'No, we'd better hang up before I really do end up in debt over this call. Just tell him I'll talk to him when I get back.'

'All right, honey. See you soon.' And with that, the conversation was ended.

The next day, after packing and having a leisurely brunch, she arrived at the airport in plenty of time to sit and stew for a good half an hour before her flight. She was the kind of person who found just the philosophy of travel tiring, even when she was simply sitting and doing nothing but reading a magazine and looking around. Flying was nothing new to her, and so she day-dreamed for most of the trip, except for a long and hilarious conversation she had with a pale, old man who sat next to her and trembled with palsy. He said the most outrageous things and had her whooping for a good half an hour, which left her feeling like a limp noodle. When the plane landed in Cincinnati, they walked out together to find their respective families.

His was the first they spotted, and they parted with the cheerful, affectionate indifference which is so unique to travelling companions, before she continued to search for some sign of Herb. She'd had it fixed so firmly in her mind that her father was picking her up that she looked at Jason twice before realising that he was watching her with a quiet, twisted smile. Her face reflected her deep surprise, and then he was coming towards her in long, graceful, eye-catching strides.

He was dressed in nothing special. Faded jeans hugged his lean hips and thighs, and a light blue shirt was open at his neck and rolled up at his elbows, bringing out the gold highlights in his hair and skin and making his eyes seem more vividly brilliant than ever. There was nothing especially outstanding about his appearance, and yet heads turned to watch him go by. Robbie didn't even see the appreciative glances other women threw at him. All she saw was Jason.

'Hello. I suppose we have to get your luggage, hm?' he said, as ordinary as he'd ever been with her, and her spirits plummeted. So it was to be a cheerful indifference from him, and she was left completely alone as she struggled to cope with her deep, surging feelings for him.

'Yes,' she said too brightly, and she whirled to find the conveyor-belt upon which the luggage from their flight was unceremoniously dumped. 'What happened to Dad?'

Jason's light eyes were on the moving luggage, his lean face preoccupied, and her spirits sank even lower. 'Hm? Oh, he was going out this evening with Marjorie, so I said I'd pick you up to save him time.' With a quickly flicked, smiling glance, he remarked, 'I didn't think it was possible, but you're darker than ever. Herb told me you got sunburned.'

'Yes, the weather was fabulous.' She hardly knew what she said, and her large suitcase almost went by before she saw it and made a darting grab.

'I think it must have been the swimming that did
it. I was in the water for several hours that first
day, and isn't water supposed to reflect sunlight?'

'I believe so. Is that it, then? We might as well
go. Here, let me take that for you.' His lean fingers
brushed hers as he took the suitcase handle, and
she nearly dropped the luggage before he had a
grip on it.

The drive back was full of pleasant, nondescript,
empty conversation. Jason informed her that he
was back at work, to which she replied that it was
a shame he hadn't had more time off. She stared
out the window and felt deadened inside while he
traced the long-familiar route back home. He
pulled into their cul-de-sac, parked in the
Morrows' driveway, and carried her suitcase again
as he walked her back to her house.

For some reason, walking into the empty house
with Jason silent and somehow distant right
behind her made her start to shake. She entered
breezily and walked right through the entire
downstairs as though she was inspecting the place,
but in reality, she was running away. The rooms
were scrupulously clean, and in the kitchen she
turned to laugh at Jason who had set down her
suitcase and followed her. He leaned against the
archway to the hall, regarding her steadily.

'Dad said the house was a wreck, but I think it
looks terrific! He must have stayed up late last
night cleaning!' she exclaimed, and then she
whirled to the kitchen counter. 'Want a cup of
coffee? I think I'll make a pot.'

'Why did you leave like that?' he asked softly,
and a terrible apprehension seized her. She turned

to stare at him and found that she'd been wrong, horribly wrong, for under his pleasant cheerfulness had burned a hot anger the entire time. It was a hard shock, for she'd never realised how adept he was at concealing his emotions.

'I needed a holiday,' she said, her voice strained. She couldn't bear to look into his hard expression and angry eyes, and so she turned back to the coffee pot and took it in her hands. All intention of making coffee had fled, and she just stared down blankly at the empty pot.

'You were already having a holiday. Why did you leave like that?' His quiet, soft voice, that frightening control, that relentlessness, sent her into a panic.

'I needed to get away.' Her words throbbed.

'You didn't say a word to me, not a word. You were gone, and I didn't find out until I came over that evening and Herb told me. You just left. I understood that you might have needed to get away, but how the hell could you have just picked up and left like that?' Though he tried, the burning heat came through the fabric of his words until his last question was savage with it.

'I couldn't face you,' she whispered, and she didn't think he could hear.

'My God,' he said deeply, and he began to swear. She whirled, feeling a little like a spinning top, and she stared at him, shocked by his molten eyes, his clenched hands, his taut, darkened expression. When he finally fell silent, they stared at each other across the distance of the room. She was weak with weariness at her intense emotions, and she bent her head to cover her eyes with one hand. Then Jason asked, his voice raw, 'What did I do to send you away?'

'It wasn't you!' she cried out. 'It was me, so just drop it, will you?'

'I'll be damned if I will,' he said quickly, passionately, striding forward. He stopped only when she shrank against the counter, afraid of the violence of feeling he emanated. 'We're going to thrash this out, because I've had it with silence and patience and waiting, and Robbie, I can't wait any longer! Answer me!'

Bewildered by his strange words and the import he gave them, she lifted her liquid-bright gaze to his to say haltingly, 'I . . . think we should stop . . . being lovers.' He flinched as if she'd struck him across the face and went ashen under his tan. Then her tears spilled over because she knew she'd hurt him, and she had never wanted to do that. She said from the back of her throat, 'I can't take having an affair. I can't take the uncertainty and the inconstancy with a healthy attitude. Some day, I . . . I want to marry, Jason . . .'

'God damn you,' he said hoarsely, his mouth distorted out of its usual beauty. Her face crumbled and she sobbed harshly into her hand. In the next instant he had her by the shoulders and was shaking her. She cried out and caught a flashing, blurred sight of his agonised eyes before he let her go and turned away to lean his forehead against his fist, taking great gulps of air as though he was suffocating. Then his head came up. His voice was underscored with bitterness as he began, 'Well. If that's what you want . . .'

'It was Linda!' she blurted, out of control. She

could never hold anything back from him. She always spilled herself out, and then shivered with the nakedness. 'I . . . saw her come over to your house that evening before I left. You came outside and hugged her, and then you both went indoors.'

His head snapped up, and he turned to stare at her incredulously. 'That's why you went? You were jealous of Linda?'

'No. Yes,' she said miserably, and then with an impatient shake of her head, she qualified, 'In a way, yes, I was jealous. But I soon realised how silly I was to be jealous of her when you had just made love to me that very day.'

'Wonders never cease.' She winced at his harsh tone.

'Please don't be cruel,' she whispered. 'Not you, of all people.'

At that, he looked away blindly. 'I feel like slapping you,' he said as though it was torn from him. 'So, just try to be glad I'm resorting to words. Do you want to know why she came over? She'd fallen in love with Ian and she saw him with another woman. It really messed her up. She came over and stayed late into the night just talking to me.'

In a flashing image, she remembered Ian's call to her that very evening, and a surge of compassion swept over her for the other woman. 'Is she all right?' she asked, hushed, and he made a quick, impatient gesture with one hand without replying. Then she tried to explain herself, saying, 'Jason, it wasn't Linda who scared me. It was my jealousy that scared me, and that's why I went. I'd never imagined that this would get so deep. We've got to stop now before we get hurt any more than . . .'

'All right!' he shouted violently, as though he couldn't bear to hear her say any more. 'All right, damn it!' He turned his face back to her, and she knew she'd never forget the sight of a single tear that splashed down his face. She reeled. 'I've had it. I've tried and tried, but you just don't get it, do you? Robbie, I've been telling you that I love you in so many ways, I don't even know how to say it anymore! Sometimes I didn't know why I bothered, but I hung on to any chance I could that you'd grow to love me back. Now I can see that it's just no use, is it?'

Her body shook so that she could hardly stand. Her heart had stopped totally for one frozen moment before pounding in slow, hard, painful strokes that roared in her ears and eyes and temples until she thought she might pass out. 'You never told me!' she cried, reaching to the counter with one hand. 'You always said you loved me, but you never said you were in love with me!'

'It was so obvious. Everybody but you knew,' he whispered, his eyes and face naked with his pain. 'Marilyn, Herb, my parents, everybody. But you never guessed. I've been in love with you all my life. I was in love with you when I left for college, but all you saw was good old Jason! And all I could do was leave and wait for you to grow up before I could see whether or not I really had a chance. But you still haven't grown up.'

'You're wrong,' she choked, shaking her head so that wet drops flew. One tear hit him, and he flinched, putting his fingers to the spot as though touching a wound and being amazed that it bled.

A calm descended over him then with a terrible finality that she sensed. She held out her hand to him and drew in a breath with which to speak, but he was already saying, 'I'm sorry I shouted at you and hurt you the way I did.' His voice was, incredibly, gentle. His face was still wet but he didn't seem to notice as he stared at her for a long, long time. His mouth was thinned to a white line. 'I don't know what else to do, Robbie,' he said quietly. 'I've been your closest friend. I've waited years to be your lover, and I thought that surely you would guess the truth when I confessed that to you. I . . . I've done nothing but picture this scene for years, but somehow we were together in the end and looking forward to spending the rest of our lives together.' Then he gave a little laugh, as if at the foolishness of young dreams. 'I suppose,' he whispered, 'I should have expected this. It was just that towards the end you seemed to change. But when I thought you had, you never did. You never saw. Maybe in time, you could have learned to love me a little. But I don't have any more time. There are some things that I can't stand either, Robbie, and . . . I love you too much to be able to stand by and wait any longer while you fall in love and marry someone else.' He reached out and cupped her cheek for a moment. 'I just wish you'd realised what I'd been trying to say. It's my fault. I didn't say it clearly enough.'

He walked away.

She stood and stared after him, and she thought, my God, he's leaving me. This is it, this is really it. He just said goodbye, and I couldn't say a thing back.

Suddenly in her mind's eye, she saw a younger Jason saying a laughing goodbye to a younger Robbie. He had looked at her lingeringly while she had stubbornly refused to give in to emotion and stared away, jaw clenched. She was angry because he was leaving without her, and he would be gone for four years to college, and to a new life. 'Goodbye, Rob,' he had said then very quietly, and she hadn't replied. She had been too busy salvaging her own pride and dignity. She knew now that he had been looking, eagerly, for some sign of grief at his departure, but she hadn't shown a thing.

She had been blind, so blind, and the only thing that astonished her as much as her own incredible blindness was his incredible patience. In retrospect, he had given her part of himself whenever she had needed it, and he had kept giving and giving while she greedily took everything.

A harsh sob sounded from her, but he was already in the hall. If his steps faltered at the sound she couldn't hear it, for she was wrapping her arms around herself and letting go of the grief she hadn't been able to at that first parting. Then she'd been sure he would be back, even though she'd been desolate at his departure. Now she knew that he wouldn't, that this was forever, and she couldn't take it. The thought of years upon years flashed in her mind. How could she make them anything but empty without him? Her future was as barren as her past had been without him, for she'd been waiting all this time for Jason to come home, she just hadn't realised it.

Something deep and elemental and soul-shaking stirred to sluggish life inside her. Something awakened that had lain dormant all this time, and it went past all life-goals and ambitions and dreams. A powerful awareness came to light inside her, a realisation of what she had carried in her heart for years but hadn't known.

She stumbled through the house. Falling out of the front door, she searched with her head slewing wildly and found Jason walking away, his head bent, his shoulders slumped. 'Jason,' she said, and the word was barely more than a whisper.

He stopped dead.

'Please don't leave me again.' He whirled, and they stared across the distance of the lawn at each other. 'I couldn't bear it a second time!'

He took three rapid steps and then halted. 'Robbie,' he said, and in his voice she heard him pleading.

'I love you,' she told him, and he raced back to haul her fiercely into his arms. His whole body trembled, and she slung her arms around his neck as he buried his face in her shoulder. 'I love you. I'm in love with you. I don't know how I couldn't have seen it before, but I do, I do . . .'

His head had lifted, and he stared down at her with eyes that blazed. 'Shut up,' he said, but she didn't take offence. Indeed, she didn't even notice and kept jabbering at him incoherently in an effort to explain the history and enormity of her feelings all at once. She only quietened when he took her mouth hungrily with his own and plunged deep into a hot kiss that sent a powerful wave of sexual yearning through her body. He dragged himself away and stared down at her. 'How the hell am I supposed to kiss you when you keep chattering like that?'

Robbie realised that they were standing on the front porch, in full sight of anyone passing in the street, and she immediately drew back. 'Let's go inside now,' she mumbled.

'What's wrong?' He looked around and then started to laugh, deeply, joyously, infuriatingly. 'I see what the problem is. You're embarrassed to kiss in public, aren't you?'

She struggled to pull out of his arms, feeling her cheeks grow hot, but he wouldn't let her go so she collapsed to hide her face in his chest. His hand came up to cup the back of her head, and she felt his lips in her hair. She felt so utterly surrounded by the way his arms so gently held her that she began to cry.

'What's this?' he asked, astonished. He bundled her back into the house and shut the door. Then he tried to tilt her face up so that he could look at her, but she resisted furiously until he fell back to stroking at her sleek brown head with such tenderness that she cried even harder. 'Oh God, Robbie, stop that. I can't stand to hear you cry like that. What's wrong, love?'

Her hands twisted into his shirt, and her face felt hot and wet with crying. With a hard quick shake of her head, she tried to avoid answering right then, but he insisted, and so she whispered, 'I just . . . I've just felt so empty and hollow these last few years. I kept searching for something to fill the void, but I couldn't care enough about anything to make a real effort. I thought something was wrong with me, but it was you. I was missing you.'

His hand passed over her hair again. 'You're the love of my life,' he murmured softly. 'And I never want to let you go, or leave again. I want to grow old with you and share the sum total of my years and myself. I want to be your lover and your best friend, and . . . Robbie, I want so much. I'm afraid to go any further. Please, be very sure.'

She drew back and traced every feature of his face with her eyes. There was such a look of love and longing in his eyes that she had to swallow before she could answer him. That look called to her heart. 'I've never been so sure of anything in my life,' she replied gently.

A vast relief crossed his features then, and he closed his eyes. She knew she'd never get tired of looking at his face, just looking. She would know that lean, beloved face in all life's aspects. A great contentment grew in her as she looked ahead to their ageing. Through the years she could see how the richness of their relationship would build until it would resemble a rare tapestry. They would share the future as they had shared the past, through disappointments and joys, through quarrels and misunderstandings and deep happiness, and their love would grow as they grew until even the bad would be good, as long as they went through it together.

He had always called to her. She realised that now. Voices from the past sang in her memory. 'Hey, Robbie, what's the matter, are you all right? Hey, Robbie, come over here and see this . . . Look! Did you see it? I think it was a hawk . . . I'm going to miss you. You're my best friend . . . Don't cry, it's going to be all right. I promise . . . I'm so in love with you, Robbie. I want to be your lover and grow old with you . . . Want to play catch outside?—Hey, Robbie . . .'

Harlequin Presents

Coming Next Month

927 AN ELUSIVE MISTRESS Lindsay Armstrong
An interior designer from Brisbane finally finds a man to share the rest of her life with—only to have her ex-husband return and reawaken feelings she'd thought were hidden forever.

928 ABODE OF PRINCES Jayne Bauling
In mysterious Rajasthan, Fate prompts a young woman to redefine her understanding of love and friendship. But the man she meets and loves will hear nothing of her breaking her engagement for him.

929 POPPY GIRL Jaqueline Gilbert
Dreams of wealth don't overwhelm a prospective heiress. But a certain Frenchman does. If only she didn't come to suspect his motives for sweeping her off her feet.

930 LOVE IS A DISTANT SHORE Claire Harrison
A reporter with a knack for getting to the heart of the matter disturbs the concentration of a young woman planning to swim Lake Ontario. Surely she should concentrate on one goal at a time.

931 CAPABLE OF FEELING Penny Jordan
In sharing a roof to help care for her boss's niece and nephew, a young woman comes to terms with her inability to express love. Is it too late to change the confines of their marriage agreement?

932 VILLA IN THE SUN Marjorie Lewty
Villa Favorita is the private paradise she shared with her husband—until his fortunes plummeted and he drove her away. Now she has been asked to handle the sale. Little does she know how closely her husband follows the market.

933 LAND OF THUNDER Annabel Murray
The past is a blank to this accident victim. She feels a stranger to her "husband." Worse, their new employer touches something disturbing within her. Something's terribly wrong here.

934 THE FINAL PRICE Patricia Wilson
In Illyaros, where her Greek grandfather lies ill, her ex-husband denies both their divorce and her right to remarry. Yet he was unfaithful to her! No wonder she hasn't told him about the birth of their son.

Available in November wherever paperback books are sold, or through Harlequin Reader Service:

In the U.S.
P.O. Box 1397
Buffalo, N.Y.
14240-1397

In Canada
P.O. Box 2800, Postal Station A
5170 Yonge Street
Willowdale, Ontario M2N 6J3